# THE SHADOW OF VENUS

# THE SHADOW OF VENUS

A CLAIRE REYNIER MYSTERY

Judith Van Gieson

WHEELER
CHIVERS

This Large Print edition is published by Wheeler Publishing, Waterville, Maine USA and by BBC Audiobooks, Ltd, Bath, England.

Published in 2004 in the U.S. by arrangement with NAL Signet, a member of Penguin Group (USA) Inc.

Published in 2004 in the U.K. by arrangement with the author.

U.S. Hardcover 1-58724-695-3 (Hardcover)
U.K. Hardcover 1-4056-3036-1 (Chivers Large Print)
U.K. Softcover 1-4056-3037-X (Camden Large Print)



The text of this Large Print edition is unabridged.
Other aspects of the book may vary from the original edition.

Set in 16 pt. Plantin by Ramona Watson.

Printed in the United States on permanent paper.

**British Library Cataloguing-in-Publication Data available**

**Library of Congress Cataloging-in-Publication Data**

Van Gieson, Judith, 1941–
The shadow of Venus : a Claire Reynier mystery / Judith Van Gieson.
p. cm.
ISBN 1-58724-695-3 (lg. print : hc : alk. paper)
1. Reynier, Claire (Fictitious character) — Fiction.
2. Homeless women — Crimes against — Fiction.
3. Abused women — Crimes against — Fiction. 4. Women librarians — Fiction. 5. Rare books — Fiction. 6. New Mexico — Fiction. 7. Large type books. I. Title.
PS3572.A42224S47 2004
13′.54—dc28 2004045833

For Phyllis Bosco, Lincoln Hansel —
You are the stars who light my sky.

# Acknowledgments

Many thanks to the Ladies of the Annex and to published poet and former *Albuquerque Journal* correspondent Patty Ann Byrum for letting me enter their lives. Maria Senaida Velasquez Huerta, Carol McGinnis Kay, and Gérard Kosicki were kind enough to read the manuscript and give me their expert advice. I'm grateful to Don Bullis for sharing his knowledge of the law and to Lawton Davis for the use of his name. As for the girls who opened their hearts and told me their stories, I couldn't have written this book without you.

# Chapter One

The Chilean poet was ending a long and distinguished career by spending a semester as a visiting professor of literature at the University of New Mexico. Librarian Claire Reynier had arranged for him to give a reading in the Willard Reading Room, a beautiful setting with high ceilings supported by vigas, windows facing onto the cactus garden, and her favorite rare books locked into bookcases on the north and south walls. The poet was a small, dignified man with a thick white mustache. Claire had been having a good hair day, but she felt too tall as she stood next to him at the podium under the glow of an overhead light. She glanced around the room and was delighted to see that all the seats had been filled.

"It gives me a great deal of pleasure to introduce Jorge Balboa," she said. "He's the author of numerous award-winning books and will read from his most recent, *Recuerdos de Amor.*"

"Thank you," Jorge replied. "You are very gracious." He lifted Claire's hand and gave it a kiss.

She left him at the podium and walked

down the aisle feeling like a butterfly had touched her hand, thinking she would stand in front of the rear bookcase since she saw no available seats. A woman in an aisle chair in the last row motioned to her. Claire paused. The woman removed a plastic bag from the adjacent seat, placed it on her lap, and slid over, giving the aisle seat to Claire.

"Thank you," Claire said as she sat down.

"You're welcome," the woman whispered. "You look beautiful today."

"Me?"

"Yes." The woman nodded.

"That's a lovely compliment." Claire felt herself blush.

"I meant it."

Claire took a closer look at the woman, who appeared young enough to be a student. Students came and went and it was harder to remember them as time went by. This woman looked vaguely familiar, but there was nothing exceptional about her to jumpstart Claire's memory. She had good bones and might have been considered pretty if her face had had more animation. Her thin brown hair fell in a straight line to her shoulders. Her clothes were beige and lavender, pale and neat, protective coloring that made her nearly invisible. If Claire had met her before, she couldn't remember when or where.

Jorge Balboa began to read in a rich baritone voice, muffled somewhat by his mustache. Although he was small in stature, his voice was operatic. The room settled into a reverent silence. Claire closed her eyes and let the words massage her back and shoulders. They were words of gentle love, love without the raw edges of anger or betrayal, love as experienced by a mature and contented man.

"You are the green and blue at twilight," Jorge said. "The silvery scimitar of the newest moon."

"Shit. That ain't poetry." A woman's voice broke in like scratchy slivers of glass.

*"Te amo, te amo mucho, te amo siempre."* Jorge ignored the interruption or was too deep in his romantic trance to notice. His voice dropped to a dramatic whisper. The audience leaned forward to hear.

"You want to hear poetry? I'll give you some poetry." Claire turned around and saw a woman standing in the back doorway. It was Ansia, a street person who hung out in the library. The campus police ignored her until she nodded out in a reading room and snored too loud or woke up and got into an argument. Ansia had extreme moods — manic or nearly comatose. Her hair was streaked the color of cherry Jell-O. Her dress was in tatters. Her feet wrapped in flimsy sandals were as rough and cracked as elephant hide.

"*Mi chiva, mi negro, mi* BB," she crooned.

"*Te amo, te amo mucho, te amo siempre. Mi jeringa, mi sancho,* my candy man. You got me all tore up from the floor up. Now that's poetry."

Claire felt Ansia had woken her from a warm and lovely dream. She'd left the rear door open to let some air into the room. As she stood up, hoping to close it and somehow persuade Ansia to leave, two uniformed campus police came around the corner, grabbed Ansia by the arms and yanked her out of the doorway. They began escorting her down the Great Hall in the direction of the main entrance. The back of her skirt was stained with menstrual blood, a sight that provoked a primal, paralyzing fear in Claire.

"Move it." A campus policeman pulled Ansia.

The man's touch set her off. "Get your goddamn bear claw hands off of me," she screamed. "I live in this state. I have the right to speak. I have the right to use the library."

*"Te amo,"* Jorge whispered. *"Mi corazón. Te amo."*

The woman who had relinquished her seat jumped up and grabbed Claire's arm. "She hates men," she said. "Make them let go of her. Please." Her eyes had the panic of a wild animal seeing the doors of a cage slam shut. She bolted through the doorway clutching her plastic bag in her arms.

Claire thought she might be going to help Ansia, but the woman turned in the opposite direction, scurrying away toward the rear exit, leaving Claire to think she should go to Ansia's aid herself, but she didn't know what she could do.

The campus police turned the corner with Ansia squirming and kicking between them. Claire closed the door and returned to her seat; her job was to supervise Jorge Balboa's reading. His gentle words of love seemed out of place now in a room that reeked of fear, but then, Claire reflected, love as she had known it had often had an element of fear.

# Chapter Two

A maintenance man discovered the body when he unlocked a storage room in the basement of Zimmerman Library on Tuesday morning after the long Memorial Day weekend. By the time Claire got to the Center for Southwest Research at nine, all the staff was buzzing about it. Knowing that the best source of information for anything that happened on campus was her colleague Celia Alegria, Claire went to her office.

Celia wore a black dress today. Since there had been a death over the weekend, it seemed like a prescient choice, although on Celia black wasn't somber. She enlivened it with lots of turquoise jewelry.

"What happened?" Claire asked her.

"Paul Begala in maintenance found a body in a storage room." Celia tapped the floor with the toe of her shoe for emphasis. "Right under here. It was a woman who hasn't been identified yet."

"A homeless person?" Homeless people and impoverished students slept in secluded nooks all over the university. One of those students had eventually become a successful script writer and a model for all those with no permanent address. It used to be that when librarians came to work in the morning they smelled breakfast cooking in the tunnels under the building. But that problem should have been solved by the new security system.

"Did you have someone in mind?" Celia asked.

"Ansia."

"Why?"

"She was evicted last week during the Jorge Balboa reading. I wish I'd done something to help her."

"Like what?"

"I don't know. Told the campus police not to be so rough. Ansia lives a dangerous life. She might have gone into the storage room to sleep and hide over the weekend."

"Which raises the question of how she got in." It was Celia's job to assign and protect the security codes that gave people access to the elevator that led to the basement and the stacks. The same security system guarded the rooms where rare manuscripts and books were stored and allowed only staff to enter and leave the library after hours. Celia gave a code to staff members and graduate students who needed one, changing the numbers periodically as staff came and went.

"Let's hope the police find that out," Claire said.

"Let's hope," Celia replied without conviction.

"How did the woman die?" Claire asked.

"The police haven't had time to do an autopsy yet, but there was heroin in the room. Most likely she OD'd."

The police didn't get to Claire's office until Wednesday afternoon when a detective named Francine Owen showed up. Her hair was streaked with gray and she wore it pulled up tight like she was trying to give a lift to a tired chin. She had the plump body of a pampered pet, but her eyes had a feral watchfulness.

"Do you have some time to talk?" she asked Claire.

"Of course."

"Good." Detective Owen settled into a chair.

"Is this about the woman in the basement?" Claire asked.

"Yes."

"Have you identified her?"

"No."

"Then it's not Ansia?"

"No. The woman we found did not resemble her and Ansia has been seen on Central since the body was discovered. We're calling the victim Jane Doe. She had a pocketful of twenty-dollar bills. Her plastic bag contained a change of clothes, a toothbrush, a comb, and baby wipes. We found nothing to identify her — no credit cards, no driver's license, no voter registration, zip, nada. Even the labels had been ripped from her clothes. We were wondering if you could help us."

"How could I help?" Claire asked.

"I have a photo of the deceased. Would you take a look?"

Claire didn't relish looking at a picture of a dead person, but she assumed she had no choice. "All right," she said.

Owen handed over the photograph. The woman's face was pale and devoid of expression, as if she had been floating in water for days and any trace of feeling had been washed away. The watery thoughts brought back a more distant memory.

"I may have talked to her once about a year ago by the duck pond," Claire said, remembering a white face coming out of the growing darkness. "It was evening and the Venus-Jupiter conjunction was visible in the sky. The woman pointed it out to me and said, 'Venus is brighter than most people realize, so bright it casts a shadow. It's visible in the daytime, too, to those who have eyes to see. I know. I've seen it.' Then she walked away. It was getting dark. I didn't get a good look at her." Claire stared at the photo. "It could be this woman."

"Do you have any idea who she was?"

"No, but I talked to her again last week at the Jorge Balboa reading in the Willard

Reading Room. She acted as if she recognized me."

"Who is Jorge Balboa?" Owen returned a wandering strand of hair to her tight hairdo.

"A Chilean poet," Claire said. "I arranged a reading for him. It was free and open to anyone who wanted to attend. Ansia came to the doorway and shouted out her own poetry until the campus police took her away."

Detective Owen smiled. "Ansia has become a poet? What did she have to say?"

"Something about her *chiva,* her BB, her *jeringa,* her candy man."

"She's an addict. Those words mean heroin, syringe, connection."

"She also said, 'You got me all tore up from the floor up.' "

"That means she's using. Did you know that the word *ansia* means heroin on the street?"

"I thought it was Spanish for anxiety," Claire said.

"It also means longing and desire. Addicts love heroin more than sex, food, shelter — more than life itself. When all their other veins are gone, they'll find a car mirror on the street and shoot up in their eyeballs. Heroin killed Jane Doe. What did she say when you talked to her last week? Anything that could help us identify her?"

"She was sitting alone near the back of the room. She had a plastic bag on the chair beside her. She picked it up and moved over to make room for me. Her looks and her dress were subdued. She would have been quite pretty if she'd made some effort. She wasn't someone I would have particularly noticed, until she told me I looked beautiful." Claire felt embarrassed to admit this.

Office Owen smiled as if she remembered what it felt like to be called beautiful. She smoothed her hair. "How sweet," she said. "It sounds like she recognized you, then."

"It's possible."

"Did she have a plastic bag when you saw her at the duck pond?"

Claire revisited her memory. "She might have."

"That's one sign of a homeless person. We're checking the shelters to see if anyone can identify her. We think she went into the storage room to shoot up and sleep."

"How did she get in? You need to punch in a code to use the elevator. You have to be a graduate student doing research at the center or a staff member to get the code."

"We're looking into that and showing the photograph around to see if anyone can ID her."

"Has the autopsy been completed yet?"

"Yes. Jane Doe died of an overdose of China White heroin. It's a West Coast drug, better quality than we usually see on the street in Albuquerque. Whenever something very pure or very strong shows up we see more deaths."

"I wouldn't have thought the woman I talked to was an addict. She was so quiet and neat."

"Jane Doe had needle tracks in her arms and she had twenties, the price of a BB."

"That's the currency you get from an ATM machine," Claire pointed out.

"It's unlikely the money came from an ATM machine. Jane Doe wasn't carrying a card."

"I'm curious. Do the police consider an overdose a murder or a suicide?" Claire asked.

"Any unattended death is treated as a homicide. The only prints we found were the victim's. If it was a suicide, she left no note to prove it."

"Would that make the person who sold or gave her the China White a murderer?"

"It might, but it would be difficult to prove. There are other means of putting dealers in jail." Detective Owen consulted her notes. "I understand that you work with rare books."

"I do," Claire replied, wondering what on earth that had to do with the death of Jane Doe.

"We found this in the room with the body." Detective Owen handed over a book-sized illustration encased in a protective plastic cover.

Claire felt her lunch lurching inside her stomach. "Oh, no."

"You recognize this?"

"It's from the book *Ancient Sites* by the explorer Thomas Duval with illustrations by the expedition artist Quentin Valor. They were the first Europeans to visit many of the sacred sites in the Southwest. Valor sketched Chaco Canyon, Canyon de Chelly, and Mesa Verde among other places. This particular illustration is of Spiral Rocks in southern Colorado." Claire loved Valor's work and thought it was a tragedy there was so little of it. "Quentin Valor had a short, adventurous life and was shot to death in a barroom brawl when he was thirty-three."

The artist's illustrations were full of exquisite detail, but they also captured the mystery and magnificence of the sacred sites. There were two pinnacles at Spiral Rocks spun into shape by eons of wind and water. A chasm several feet wide had developed between them. That was how they would stand and how they would remain until eventually they disintegrated and turned to dust. Twins. Always together. Always apart.

"Does the library have this book?" Detective Owen asked.

"We did," Claire said. "It was down the hall in the Anderson Reading Room. We had a pristine first edition."

"Is it valuable?"

"Intact it's worth several thousand dollars. With pages removed, it's worth less. I'd say the illustration alone is worth two hundred dollars."

"Could this Jane Doe have been stealing illustrations from the library and selling them for drugs?"

It was something Claire hated to even consider, but it was a definite possibility. "See how straight this edge is?" She pointed. "The illustration was very carefully razor-bladed out of the book. It could be the work of a professional. It doesn't look like the work of an addict."

"Can you show me the book?" Detective Owen asked.

"I hope so," Claire replied.

She took Owen to the Anderson Reading Room, where even a detective had to show ID before being admitted. She went to a balcony shelf and was pleased to find *Ancient Sites* exactly where it was supposed to be. Claire lifted the book from the shelf, checked the index for Spiral Rocks, and turned to the page. Her stomach lurched again when she discovered a smooth edge where the illustration had once been. Detective Owen placed her illustration beside it and one razor-bladed edge connected with another in a perfect fit. Claire turned to the other illustrated pages in the book and was relieved to see them all in place.

"Maybe she began with Spiral Rocks intending to work her way through the book," Owen said.

"If I were gutting this book for drug money, Spiral Rocks wouldn't be my first choice," Claire replied. She showed Detective Owen the Chaco Canyon illustrations, which were even more magnificent than the one of Spiral Rocks. Chaco Canyon was a vast and important ruin created for purposes that still weren't understood. Spiral Rocks was small and intimate in comparison, created by the forces of nature and not by man.

"Those rocks look like . . . you know what," Detective Owen said.

Claire knew. The Southwest was full of rocks that resembled erect penises. "I don't think that's why Jane Doe cut this illustration out," she said. "Maybe Spiral Rocks represented something to her. If she traded it for China White, you wouldn't have found both the illustration and the drugs in the storage room, would you?"

"Unless she traded something else for the China White and planned to trade Spiral Rocks the next time she needed to shoot up."

Claire's eyes circled the reading room. From floor to balcony, from balcony to ceiling, there were rows and rows of valuable books. The story of the Southwest could be found in this room. How would anyone ever establish what had been cut out of the books here? You'd have to open every book, check every page. There were thousands of books in the Anderson Reading Room and many contained artwork. "Do you think there is a drug dealer who would trade drugs for art?"

"Not at the street level, but maybe higher up. Those guys have to put their money somewhere. Why not collect art? China White is a better class of heroin than we usually see in Albuquerque. Maybe we're looking at a better class of dealer. On the other hand, Jane may have been selling artwork to another interested party and using the cash to buy drugs. She could also have been turning tricks for drug money."

"If Jane Doe was systematically looting books in the Anderson Reading Room, she had to be doing it when there was no one around, which again raises the question of how she got in. She'd need an ID in the daytime and a security code after hours."

"What about the cleaning people? Could they have let her in?"

"No one but staff cleans in the Anderson Reading Room. The security people don't have a code either. If they find that someone has left a door open, they are supposed to notify Celia Alegria."

"She's on my list," Detective Owen said.

# Chapter Three

Claire had dinner with her friend John Harlan after work and didn't get home until nine. Her house was dark and her cat, Nemesis, was waiting at the door. She fed him and went into the bathroom. When she turned on the light a flock of moths flew out of her towels and beat their wings against the light fixture. Every few years Albuquerque had a moth infestation. There was nothing to do about it but turn off the lights whenever possible and wait in the dark for them to go away. A moth settled on the windowsill, giving Claire a moment to examine it. The wings were the color of parchment and had a pattern that resembled endpapers. She knew if she touched the wings they would leave a smudge on her fingers. While the moths fluttered around the light, Claire stared at herself in the mirror. What had Jane Doe seen that made her use the word "beautiful"? Claire couldn't continue to think of the deceased as Jane Doe. She had to find another name for her. If she couldn't discover the woman's true identity, she would pick a name herself.

Claire liked the way her hair looked now

— short and curly with hairdresser highlights. She had good bones and robin's-egg blue eyes. She wasn't bad looking but it had been a long time since anyone had called her beautiful. Knowing that a joyful expression could momentarily transform most people, Claire tried to bring back the enthusiasm and the radiance she had felt when she introduced Jorge Balboa, but she couldn't do it. Her features settled into a worried frown. The moths beating against the light were distracting and she was disturbed by the things she'd learned from Detective Owen.

She turned off the light and paced her house in the dark. The compliment had been so unexpected and so pleasing she had wanted to cherish it, to bring it out of memory from time to time and polish it. She hated to think it came from a drug addict who went around the library after hours cutting illustrations out of valuable books. But until Claire examined every illustrated book the library owned or knew more about the woman, it was a fear likely to come, flapping its wings, out of the night. She didn't see the woman she met as a street person or an addict, but then how to explain the China White and the plastic bag containing a toothbrush, a change of clothes, a comb, and baby wipes? How to explain how the woman gained access to the basement and the Anderson Reading Room?

Claire had a more recent edition of *Ancient Sites*, too recent to be valuable. She went to her bedroom and shut the door, hoping to lock the moths out before she turned on the light. She took the book from her bookshelf and turned to the illustration of Spiral Rocks. In the years since the Duval exploration a great deal had been learned about the sacred sites the expedition visited, some of which — like evidence indicating there was cannibalism at Chaco Canyon — Claire would rather not know. It had been established that some buildings at Chaco Canyon were orientated toward the sun and others toward the phases of the moon. The spiral carved into Fajada Butte recorded solstices, equinoxes, and other cycles with amazing accuracy.

But little was known about Spiral Rocks. Since it was a small site, located now on private property, it hadn't been studied the way Chaco Canyon had. Claire looked at Quentin Valor's illustration of the rocks pointing toward the sky and wondered whether there was any astronomical significance to the site. Was the rock formation worshipped by the Anasazi or used by them in some way as a calendar? Jane Doe had expressed an interest in Venus. It was possible she had an interest in astronomy, too. She might even have taken courses in the subject.

A solitary moth had made its way into the bedroom and fluttered toward the light with the ardor of an addict. Claire turned off the lamp, but the moth found the warmth and beat its wings against the bulb as if it had discovered a long lost mate. The moth infestation resembled having a house full of unwelcome intruders, restless thoughts, spirits of the dead, and the unnotified next of kin.

Claire didn't sleep well, was awake at dawn and at her office by eight. She took her copy of *Ancient Sites* to work with her. Before she even sat down at her desk, Celia showed up at the door wearing a crimson dress that flattered her vivid coloring and reflected her angry mood.

"I am deeply, totally, pissed off," she said.

"About Jane Doe?"

"Yes. How in the hell did she get into the basement and into the Anderson Reading Room after hours?"

"Could she have worked here at some point or been a graduate student?" Claire asked.

"The detective showed me the photo, but I didn't recognize her. She hasn't been an employee or a student at the center since I've been here. I never gave Jane Doe a code, but somebody must have."

Claire's mood was beginning to feel like she had dressed in scratchy brown burlap. "Wouldn't someone have noticed Jane Doe if she was in the Anderson Reading Room after hours? There are security guards on duty then."

"There are, but they don't check ID. Suppose they did see Jane Doe and thought she was a grad student or a staff member. Could she have passed for one?"

"Yes. She wasn't outrageously dressed or out of control like Ansia."

"There are lots of legitimate people who work late in the Anderson Reading Room. Detective Owen is going to show the photo to the guards. Maybe one of them will remember Jane Doe. If the guards find a door open or anything out of order at night they are supposed to report it to me. Every time someone punches in a code anywhere in the center the time and date are recorded. I told Detective Owen I would go through the records and see what I could find."

"It's also possible someone carelessly left the door to the Anderson Reading Room open and Jane Doe let herself in."

"Well, then, did someone leave the elevator door to the basement open, too? You can't get into the basement without taking the elevator and the elevator won't move unless you enter a code."

"What's the room she died in like?" Claire asked. Like most people who worked at the library she avoided the utilitarian part of the basement.

Celia shrugged. "Beige. Depressing. There

isn't much in there except for empty boxes and dead roaches."

"That whole part of the basement is depressing, isn't it?"

"Some people think it's enlivened by ghosts," Celia said. "Supposedly it's haunted by the very first librarian here, who is seen from time to time wandering around in a pinafore dress."

"Have you ever seen her?" Claire asked.

"Only her shadow."

"Did Detective Owen tell you about the illustration that was cut out of *Ancient Sites*?"

"Yeah. I bet you were thrilled about that."

"I wasn't happy. I brought in my own copy," Claire said, opening it to the Spiral Rocks illustration. "It's possible Jane Doe cut out this particular illustration because it meant something to her."

"The meaning of *those* rocks is obvious, isn't it?" Celia said, raising her thick and luxuriant eyebrows.

"Maybe there's a deeper meaning."

"So to speak," Celia laughed. "Why are you so interested in Jane Doe?"

"I met her, or maybe I should say I talked to her. I was standing by the duck pond at dusk last year and she came up and pointed out the Venus-Jupiter conjunction in the evening sky. She told me Venus was so bright it could cast a shadow. She said it was visible in the daytime to those who had eyes to see.

Maybe she had an interest in astronomy or archeoastronomy."

"Maybe," Celia said. "The person here who knows the most about that subject is Lawton Davis in the Department of Earth and Planetary Sciences. You should talk to him."

"I will. I spoke to Jane Doe again at the Jorge Balboa reading," Claire continued, "when she offered me a seat. Ansia appeared in the doorway and began to recite an ode to heroin, drowning out Jorge Balboa. I got up to close the door and Jane panicked, pushed me aside, and ran out." Claire didn't repeat the "You look beautiful" remark. She felt foolish doing so in front of Celia.

"Homeless people aren't in the best of mental health," Celia said. "Maybe Jane suffered from claustrophobia."

"If she was claustrophobic, what was she doing in a locked room in the basement?"

"She didn't lock it herself," Celia said. "The storage rooms have deadbolts that can only be locked with a key. The police didn't find a key inside the room. Trust me, I asked. Paul Begala in maintenance says he always locked that door before he went home and he locked it on Friday night. He didn't realize anybody was inside, he says. When he opened it again on Tuesday morning he found Jane Doe dead. Because Detective Owen told me to, I'm going to check the records to see who used the code to get into the basement on Friday. But it won't prove anything. Any number of people could have gone down there on Friday. I pointed out to her that the elevator also stops at the stacks."

"What about the Anderson Reading Room records?"

"I'll check them, too, but I think it will be the same story. The code only needs to be used after hours, but everybody who works or studies here has a legitimate reason to use the Anderson Reading Room day or night. I have to go." Celia raised her eyes to the ceiling. "I have a meeting with Harrison."

Harrison Hough, their prickly boss, was difficult in the best of times. "I suppose he's going to get on your case about Jane Doe entering the basement."

"I suppose he is," Celia replied.

# Chapter Four

Celia returned to Claire's office just before noon, scowling in imitation of a disgruntled Harrison.

"What did he say?" Claire asked.

" 'We must get to the bottom of this.' "

"He has a knack for stating the obvious."

"I was planning to go through the records, anyway. Here's what I discovered. There were three incidents this spring when security reported to me that they found the door to the Anderson Reading Room open at night but no one inside. On all three occasions the code of a doctoral candidate named Seth Malcolm had been entered. He could easily have left the door open for Jane Doe on his way out."

"Did he use the elevator last Friday?"

"Several times. The last entry was at five p.m. I need to talk to Seth. He's not entitled to do his research here if he's been breaking library rules."

"I want to be there when you talk to him."

That remark elevated Celia's eyebrows. "Why?"

"I need to find out if he's responsible for the stolen illustration."

"Do you know him?"

"We've met." Claire remembered Seth as a lanky, preppy-looking student with long bangs and a nervous gesture of shaking them out of his eyes.

"He's writing his dissertation on Tobiah James, and that gives him access to the stacks, the Anderson Reading Room, and everyplace else in the library."

Claire knew Tobiah James as an Easterner of independent means who wandered New Mexico in the early twentieth century studying the Pueblo Indians, sketching, and taking voluminous notes.

They discussed where to meet Seth. Claire was in favor of somewhere far away from campus where they wouldn't run into anybody they knew.

"But then I'd have to explain why I want to see him," Celia said. "I want to surprise him with what I know."

"What about Detective Owen? Won't she want to talk to him?" Claire asked.

"Sure, but I want to do it first. As Harrison just reminded me, supervising the codes is my responsibility. It's my job that's on the line here. We'd be better off hiding in plain sight someplace nearby. Then Seth won't suspect it's a big deal. He'll think I'm just assigning him a new code. How about the Frontier?"

It was a popular restaurant right across

Central from the university. "All right," Claire said.

Celia left a note in Seth's box asking him to meet her there the following afternoon. She and Claire arrived on time, sat at the window, and watched the street life pass by on Central while they waited for Seth to show up. As the time dragged on Claire asked Celia how she would interpret Seth's tardiness.

Celia's voice was acerbic with sarcasm. "Let me see. He got wrapped up in his work and forgot? He doesn't wear a watch? He thinks his time is more valuable than ours? He's a space case? He doesn't want to meet me because he's feeling guilty or embarrassed?"

"Is he a New Mexican?" Claire asked. New Mexicans were known for their elastic sense of time. Trying to get two New Mexicans together could take all day.

"No. He's from the East," Celia replied. "He got his B.A. in American Studies from Boston University."

"What brought him to UNM?"

"He got a fellowship to pursue a doctorate on Tobiah James. James was also from the East. Maybe Seth felt a connection. His advisor told me that he hasn't been doing his work and is in danger of losing his fellowship."

"He's been seen doing research, hasn't he?"

"He's been spending time in the library, but he hasn't been turning in his papers."

"Which raises the question of whether he was doing something else in the library."

"Like stealing illustrations?" Celia asked.

"It's possible," Claire said.

While Celia poured sugar into her espresso, Claire looked out the window and noticed Seth dodging traffic as he crossed the street. In the carnival atmosphere of Central Avenue, he looked alien in his khakis and white shirt with the collar open and the sleeves buttoned at the wrist. His preppy way of dressing made him stand out, reminding Claire of the way Jane Doe's pallid neatness made her stand out. Their very inconspicuousness made them conspicuous. Claire watched Seth slouch as he walked with his head down and his hands in his pockets. The mother in her wanted to admonish him to straighten up.

"Here he comes," she said to Celia.

"At that speed it'll be another twenty minutes before he gets inside," Celia replied. She went to the door and waved to Seth. When he didn't respond, she yelled at him. He looked up and quickened his pace.

After he entered the restaurant he went to the counter, got himself a Coke, and brought it over to the table. Before he sat down he took off his backpack and put it on the floor.

His bangs separated as he bent over to sip the Coke, revealing a premature white streak in his mouse brown hair.

Celia introduced Claire.

"We've met, haven't we?" he asked. "Aren't you the rare-book expert?"

"Yes."

"What's this about?" he asked Celia. "Are you assigning me a new code?"

"Have you heard about the woman who was found dead in the storage room?"

"Yeah. Sure. Of course. Hasn't everybody?"

"Did you know her?"

"She hasn't been identified. So how could I say whether I knew her or not?"

"I'll ask the investigating officer to show you her photo," Claire said.

Seth's eyes widened as if the words "investigating officer" had set off an alarm. He turned back to his Coke and it gurgled as he sucked on the straw.

"I met Jane Doe," Claire said. "I can describe her if that would help you to identify her."

"Sure. Why not?" Seth said.

"She was in her late teens or early twenties. Her hair was thin and brown, shoulder length, very straight. She had high cheekbones and would have been quite striking if she had tried to be. She wore a pale dress on the occasions I saw her. Her appearance and demeanor were quiet and unobtrusive."

Seth's eyes darted from Claire to Celia like a moth seeking the warmest place to light. Eventually they settled on the woman who had asked the question — Claire.

"I hope it wasn't her, but it sounds like Maia," he said. "She was a homeless person who hung out in the library. She told me she spent her nights at the Hope Central Shelter. She was quiet, the kind of person who could study in the same room with you all day and you'd never notice her. Once I went outside to have a cigarette. She was sitting on the steps and we started talking. She was smart, very interested in learning. She would have made an excellent student if UNM would ever have admitted her."

"Did she tell you why she was homeless?" Claire asked.

Seth shrugged. "All she ever said was that Coyote chased her and she ran away. In Greek mythology Maia is one of the seven daughters of Atlas and Pleione who became the constellation Pleiades. The sisters were pursued by Orion, the hunter, who saw them walking in the woods and fell in love with them. They escaped into the sky. Maia never told me where she came from or if that was her given name."

"What did she mean by Coyote?" Claire asked.

"I don't know."

"Did she tell you about the role Maia

played in mythology?" Claire suspected a Ph.D. candidate would want to show off his knowledge and she was right.

"She didn't have to tell me about Greek mythology," Seth said. "I already knew."

"Did you let her into the Anderson Reading Room?" was Claire's next question.

Seth shook his head and his bangs fell down across his forehead. "I wouldn't do that. If I did, I would lose my fellowship."

The records were Celia's department. Her bangle bracelets clinked as she placed her hands on the table and confronted Seth. "You checked into the Anderson Reading Room after hours on three nights this spring when security later reported to me that the door had been left open."

"I use the Anderson Reading Room at night. It's the best time for me to work. I don't remember ever using it when I was the only one there. Anybody could have forgotten to shut the door when he or she went out."

"A Quentin Valor illustration from *Ancient Sites* by Thomas Duval was found in the room with Maia. Are you familiar with that book?" Claire asked. She watched indecision play across Seth's face as if he was debating whether he wanted to appear knowledgeable or not.

Knowledge won out. "Of course," Seth said. "The book is a classic. Every student of the Southwest knows that book."

"The illustration had been very carefully cut out of the first edition in the Anderson Reading Room," Claire told him.

"Do you think Maia stole it from the library?"

"Somebody did," Claire said. "It was the illustration of Spiral Rocks. Do you have any idea why she would have that particular illustration?"

"None," Seth said. "I know nothing about Spiral Rocks."

While Claire pondered what it took for him to admit there was a subject he knew nothing about, Celia picked up the beat. "Your code was also used to enter the basement elevator at five p.m. on the day that Maia died."

Seth brushed back his hair. "I was doing research on Tobiah James. His papers are stored in the stacks. What's wrong with my going into the basement elevator?"

"Nothing," Celia said, "unless you let Maia in or gave her your code."

Seth drained his Coke and sucked on the ice. "You're not going to accuse me of that, are you?" he pleaded. "I'd lose my fellowship."

"We need to do more investigating," Celia said. Claire had never heard her use such a harsh, prosecutorial tone before.

Seth put down his Coke, picked up his backpack, and left the restaurant.

Once he was out the door Claire said,

"You were the bad cop in this investigation."

"I have to be," Celia said. "I'll lose my job if I give out the code to people who let the homeless in or steal from the library. Between you and me, I think Seth has dirt on his wings, but I'll need more evidence before I can take away his privileges."

"I don't think he'll abuse them anymore," Claire said.

"Not with Maia, anyway, now that she's dead."

"Do you think he was pretending he didn't know she was the woman who died in the storage room?"

"I think he either knew or suspected."

"If he was lying when he said he didn't know, then he could be lying about anything."

"Or everything."

"You have to wonder whether there was something sexual between Seth and Maia." Claire was glad the young woman had been given a name. Even if Maia wasn't her real name it was a name that had resonance. From now on she intended to call her Maia instead of Jane Doe.

"What do you think?" Celia asked.

"They have the same look. You'd notice them on Central but you wouldn't in the library. It's hard to say if they are just quiet people or if they're wearing a disguise."

"Usually people are attracted to their opposite, aren't they?" Celia asked. "It's more interesting than going to bed with your twin."

"But if one was hiding behind a disguise, then they could be opposites underneath," Claire said.

"True," said Celia.

"Considering the story of Maia and her sisters and the fact that Maia said Coyote chased her, it could have been abuse that put her on the street."

"Abuse puts a lot of women on the street."

"I'd like to see what the room where Maia died looks like. Can you show it to me?" Claire asked.

Celia finished her coffee and put down her cup. "Sure, if you really want to see it."

"It's not considered a crime scene and sealed off anymore, is it?"

"Was it ever?" Celia said. "A homeless woman goes into a basement and OD's, the police don't consider that a crime."

"Detective Owen told me every unattended death is treated as a homicide."

"It's just a formality. They'll check the fingerprints and the missing-persons reports. If they don't find out who Jane Doe is soon, they'll put the case on the back burner and move on to the next crime. If they do find out, they'll notify the next of kin and then they'll move on to the next crime." Celia glanced at the clock on the wall. "If you want to look at the storage room, let's do it now. I've got a meeting coming up."

# Chapter Five

They walked back across Central, the dividing line between the campus and the city. Although it was a line people could easily cross, the atmosphere was very different on the UNM side. It wasn't exactly an ivory tower, but the beauty of the architecture, art, and landscaping did provide some relief from the reality of the street. They returned to Zimmerman and went to the elevator. Claire watched while Celia punched in her code. She happened to be close enough to read the numbers, but Celia knew her. She wouldn't let someone she didn't know peer over her shoulder.

As the elevator descended the short distance to the basement Claire felt like she was entering a Plutonian underworld. The light was dim in the utilitarian part of the basement. The hallway was shadowed by overhead cables marked CHILLED WATER RETURN snaking along under the ceiling. The air-conditioning system throbbed. The only bright notes were the red EXIT signs over the doors and the crimson dress Celia wore. Claire followed her down the hall to the crime scene, which was not marked by yellow police tape or anything else. Celia turned the knob and opened the unlocked door. The room was dark until she flipped the switch. The fluorescent overhead light flickered on, illuminating a pile of empty brown boxes and a number of industrial-strength roaches that had gone belly-up on the floor. If the police had ever drawn an outline of Maia's body, it was gone now. It was hard to tell exactly where she had lain. Putting herself in the woman's shoes, Claire imagined Maia would have settled in a corner where she could see the open door without being noticed herself; then she fell asleep or passed out there. Maintenance came by, closed and locked the door. If Jane Doe woke up again, she would have felt trapped and frightened.

"We need to talk to the maintenance man who found her," Claire said.

"I'll see if I can locate him," Celia said.

"I'll wait here. Would you mind shutting the door on your way out?" Claire could have easily closed the door herself, but it wouldn't have been the same as hearing someone else click it shut.

Celia paused. "Why?"

"I want to understand Maia, to know why she came here, how it felt to be locked in this room."

"You want me to find you some heroin while I'm at it?" Celia snapped. "Do you want to know what it feels like to shoot up and OD, too?"

"Just humor me a little. Okay?"

Celia threw up her hands. "All right. I'll be right back." The door closed behind her with a small sigh of a click.

Claire doubted that was the sound Jane Doe heard, if she heard the door close at all. She imagined the door had closed on Maia with a thud that had finality, fear, possibly even death in it. Claire had seen claustrophobia often enough to know the power a closed door or a tunnel could have, but she wasn't claustrophobic herself. She didn't like being alone in the storage room with the door shut, but she didn't panic. She could open the door herself from the inside. Even if she couldn't, she knew Celia would come back. But what if Maia was a girl who'd been abused and came in here to hide? Suppose she woke up after everyone had gone for the weekend? What if she screamed and pounded on the door and no one answered? This room had the smell and taste of fear. Claire closed her eyes to see what would come out of the darkness. When that wasn't enough, she turned off the light.

She was twelve and sleeping out in a tent in her friend Susan Hogan's backyard at Hawley Lake, Arizona. When the coyotes began to yip and howl, Susan got scared and ran back to the house. But even at twelve Claire was too sensible to be afraid of coyotes. She wanted to have her outdoor experience. She remained in the tent, curled up in her sleeping bag, and went to sleep.

She woke up feeling betrayed by her own body. Her nipples were hard. There was a hand inside her sleeping bag, fondling her breast. She felt a hot breath on the back of her neck. It had to be a dream. If she escaped into the white, it would go away.

"That means you want me." The man pinched her breast. His voice was a hoarse whisper. The alcohol smell was heavy on his breath.

"Let go of me." She tried to twist away in the narrow space of the sleeping bag.

"You'll like it. I can teach you some tricks," the man said.

"Get your hands off of me." Claire kicked the sleeping bag that bound her legs like a mermaid's tail.

"Hey, it's nothing. Don't get excited, all right? I got the wrong impression. You're not the girl I thought you were. I'm leavin'. Okay?"

The man crawled out of the tent. Claire fought with the zipper as she struggled to unzip the sleeping bag. She couldn't go into Susan Hogan's house. She could not stay here. She ran through the dark with the stars lighting a path through the woods. She reached her own house and let herself in. No one ever locked their doors in Hawley Lake, but she locked the front door behind her, went upstairs to her own room, and crawled into bed. Her eyes were wide open when her mother opened the door in the morning.

"Why did you come home, dear?" her mother asked.

"Susan was afraid of coyotes and went inside. I fell asleep. I . . . I had a bad dream."

"You came home all alone in the dark?"

"Yes."

Claire's mother sat down on the bed and stroked her daughter's hair. "Why didn't you go to Susan's house and call us?"

"I couldn't do that."

"That must have been a very bad dream," her mother said.

"I dreamt a man grabbed me."

Her mother sighed. "You'll be getting your period soon. You haven't started that already, have you?"

"No."

"Get up, dear, and I'll fix you some breakfast. Your father's waiting."

"In a minute," Claire said.

After her mother left, Claire pulled the covers over her head. How could she tell her parents, Susan, or anyone else that she knew the man who had touched her in the night? He was Susan's father and her own father's friend. She got up and took a shower so hot it turned her skin blistery red. She wanted to scrub away the man's touch, his breath, his smell. She tried to scrub away his very existence.

She dressed and went down to breakfast. Her father was sitting at the table reading the newspaper, gentle and distracted as always. He worked as an engineer but he had an artist's temperament. He was happiest tending his garden or painting in his studio. Claire was her father's favorite, the apple of his eye, his bright and beautiful daughter. She didn't have the words to tell her father that his friend had fondled her. What could her father ever do to right that wrong? Go to Susan's house with his rifle, shoot George Hogan or beat him up, call the cops, have him arrested? Was her father capable of that? She would have to go to court and testify against George Hogan. Everybody would know that he had touched her. Her words could put Susan's father in prison and she would become known as "the girl who." Susan was her friend. That was what made George Hogan's act so despicable. He'd betrayed his own daughter; he'd betrayed his friend.

Claire sat down at the breakfast table, poured milk on her Rice Krispies, and listened to them crackle and pop. Her mother was in the utility room doing the laundry. The washing machine whirred. Her father smiled over the top of the paper.

"Did you lock the door when you came home last night?" he asked.

She nodded.

"Why?"

"I was afraid."

"Of what?"

"Coyotes," she said.

"You know better than to be afraid of coyotes."

"It's different in the night," Claire said.

"Well, it's daytime now. You don't have to worry about coyotes." He squeezed her hand and went back to the paper.

Claire stared at her Rice Krispies and didn't say a word about George Hogan.

Hard as it was to find the words at that moment, it became even harder as time passed and the incident became more deeply buried. She avoided George and Susan. When she had to be in their company, she looked away. She had trouble eating and sleeping. She developed anxieties, not of confinement but of exposure. The name for it was agoraphobia. There were times when it took all of Claire's teenage courage to get out of the house, when food in her stomach made her want to throw up. It was years before she talked about that night in the tent. She never talked about it to anyone who knew Susan or her own family. Sharing this room with the spirit of Maia had brought it all back.

* * *

The door opened and Celia flipped on the light. "What's the matter with you?" she asked. "You look like you saw a ghost."

"I did," Claire said.

"The librarian in the pinafore dress?"

"No. I was just imagining what Maia might have felt in here."

"I found Paul Begala. Paul, Claire Reynier."

Paul was a small wiry man dressed in a gray uniform with his name embroidered across the pocket. He had a chipped front tooth and eyes that didn't match. One was blue and one was brown. Claire felt that only the blue one focused on her. Paul's keys were on a ring attached to his belt loop and they jingled when he moved.

"Did you know the girl who died?" he asked Claire.

"I met her," Claire said. "She may have stolen valuable illustrations from the library. If I could understand why she came down here and what happened to her, it might help to identify her."

"She was homeless. The homeless come down here whenever they can find a way in. They're looking for a place to sleep or shoot up." Paul shrugged. "It's safer than being on the street."

"How do they get in?"

"Someone gives them their code or they

trade something for it. It's a hard life. Women on the street will turn a trick for a place to sleep."

"Did you ever see this woman down here before?" Claire asked, wondering if Jane Doe had ever turned a trick for him. Paul Begala was unlikely to admit it if that happened; it could cost him his job.

"I never saw her at all until I unlocked the door on Tuesday morning and found her in that corner, cold and dead as a stone with the needle on the floor." Paul's words were firm and definite, but his eyes wandered, circling the room.

"Did you see any of the staff in this part of the basement last week?" Celia asked.

"I saw one guy a couple of times, but I don't know his name."

"What did he look like?" Celia asked.

"Tall. Skinny. He has a white streak in his hair."

"Could his name have been Seth Malcolm?"

"Coulda. I didn't ask him."

"Was he in this room?"

"I didn't see him here. When I saw him he was in the hallway. He said he was going to the stacks."

"When do you lock the door?" Claire asked him.

"When I go home at night and over the weekend. It's left open during the day."

"Do you need to lock it? There doesn't seem to be anything of value in here," Claire said.

"I do it to keep the riffraff out."

Celia thanked him for his help and asked about the health of his wife, Marisa.

"She's doin' okay," he said. "I'll tell her you asked about her. She'll appreciate that. Anything else?"

"That's it for me," Celia said.

"Me, too," said Claire.

Claire heard the keys jingle as Paul turned and walked away. She and Celia went in the opposite direction and entered the elevator.

"What do you think of Paul Begala?" Claire asked her friend.

"I don't know him that well," Celia said. "I knew his wife, Marisa, better. She used to clean at night, but she got MS and she can't work anymore. It must be very difficult for Paul to care for her. He's supposed to tell me if he finds something out of the ordinary like a door that should be locked but isn't. Only he never does. I hear from the guards from time to time that something is out of order, but never from him."

"Do you think he was telling the truth when he said he never saw Maia before?" Claire asked.

"Maybe. Maybe not. Maybe he's the one who let her in. Maybe he even had sex with her. Having a sick wife could send a man looking elsewhere. Better him than Seth Malcolm, anyway. I'd hate to think it was a graduate student or one of the library staff."

"A grad student familiar with *Ancient Sites* would know that the illustrations in the book are valuable."

"True. It's also true that his work gave Seth a legitimate reason to be in the basement."

The elevator arrived and they stepped in and rode it to the main floor.

"If Paul or Seth let Maia in, he violated library policy," Celia said. "It could cost Paul his job and Seth his fellowship, but it doesn't change the fact that she died alone of a self-inflicted overdose, does it?"

The elevator door opened.

"I guess not," Claire said.

# Chapter Six

When she got home that night Claire went to the bookshelves in her bedroom to see what she had on the mythology of the constellations. She wasn't good about identifying them in the sky and even had trouble locating the Big and Little Dippers, but the Milky Way was easy. She knew that the Plateau Indians considered it to be the tracks of the dead and that it was bright enough to cast a shadow in areas removed from ambient light. Venus was easy to identify when it was the first planet in the evening sky, and Mars appeared brilliantly red when it was close to the earth. She had observed the conjunction last year and she followed the phases of the moon but that was about all Claire could identify in the night sky. She knew for sure she'd never be able to locate Venus in the daytime.

She turned on all the lights in her house to confuse the moths and divert them from the reading lamp in her bedroom. She pulled some books off the shelves and sat down to read about the stars. Claire learned that over thousands of years many cultures had observed the movement of the constellation

Pleiades and created similar mythologies involving not having a home on earth. Often the planets were siblings, usually girls but sometimes boys. As Seth had said, in Greek mythology they were the seven daughters of Atlas and Pleione: Electra, Maia, Taygeta, Alcyone, Merope, Celaeno, and Asterope. The sisters were pursued by Orion, the hunter, after he saw them walking in the woods and fell in love with them. When Zeus saw the sisters were in danger, he changed them into doves, who flew away into the sky.

In some of the myths there were only six stars or siblings. One of the stars was faint and best seen by averting the eyes and not staring at it directly. In all the myths there was an explanation for why the sisters or brothers left the earth. Often they were fleeing danger. Sometimes they danced or played too hard until they were lifted off the ground and spun into the sky. Sometimes they were happy in the sky. Sometimes they longed to return to earth. In a Kiowa myth Claire read that the girls were playing with a brother and amusing each other by pretending he was a bear. Then the brother turned into a real and voracious bear and the girls fled in fear to the sky. Claire saw that myth as a dramatization of the dangers of incest.

Another version featuring incest made Claire stop, put down her book, and stare at the wall. In this version Coyote committed incest with his daughters, forcing them to flee to the sky and turn into stars. Incest would explain why Maia became homeless, why she took her symbolic name and hid behind a pale façade, possibly even why she turned to heroin. Claire felt she couldn't put Maia to rest until she found out who she was, where she came from, and whether she had been pursued by Coyote, the predator, or Orion, the hunter. If someone had harmed her, that person had to be caught and punished.

Claire turned off all the lights and went to bed. She lay awake listening to the moths batting their wings, staking their claim on the warmth left behind in the bulbs.

After Celia had her meeting with Detective Owen and showed her the records, she sent the policewoman down the hall to Claire's office. Detective Owen seemed tired to Claire when she poked her head through the doorway. Even her upswept hairdo had begun to droop.

"Celia Alegria said you wanted to see me?" Detective Owen said.

"Yes," Claire replied. "Come in. Have a seat."

"Have you found any more missing illustrations?"

"No," Claire said. "I don't know where to

begin looking. To examine every valuable illustrated book in the library is an impossible task. It would help if I could narrow down the field. Did Celia tell you that the dead woman called herself Maia?"

"Yes, and that Seth Malcolm gave you that information and may have let the deceased into the basement. I'll be talking to him." Detective Owen eased herself into the visitor's chair as if her joints hurt.

"Have you discovered where she got the drugs? Would the dealer be able to tell you anything about her?" Claire asked.

"We haven't found the dealer. The autopsy established that most of the needle tracks and the scars on her arms were old. She didn't have the tracks between her toes of a long-term user. It looks like she used for a while, kicked, then started up again. It doesn't appear she was selling illustrations for drugs on a regular basis, if that's any help to you."

"It is," Claire said. "Have you seen any more deaths from China White?"

"No."

"Does the word 'coyote' have any meaning in the drug world?"

Owen gave a weary shrug. "Only the meaning it has everywhere else. Coyote is the smuggler who brings drugs or people across the border."

"Maia told Seth she once stayed at the Hope Central Shelter."

"We're looking into it."

"Do you think it's possible Maia was her real name?"

"Possible, although many women on the street use fictitious names; they don't want to be found."

"I did some research on the name," Claire said, "and found that in Greek mythology Maia is one of the seven daughters of Atlas and Pleione. Orion, the hunter, pursued the girls. When Zeus saw they were in danger, he changed them into doves, who flew into the sky and became the constellation Pleiades."

"Maybe you should start looking through the library's astronomy books," Detective Owen said. "We have a better chance of recovering stolen artwork if we know exactly what we're looking for."

"I thought I would start with archeoastronomy. In many of the Pleiades myths girls are fleeing abuse. It's possible Maia was abused, was hiding from her abuser, and he found her."

"Many women on the street have been abused," Detective Owen said. "And many of them turn to prostitution. They need to do it to get money to buy drugs. But then they need to be high to prostitute themselves. It's a vicious cycle. Sometimes their abusers do track them down, but it doesn't end with the woman dying alone with a needle at her side, I can tell you that. Trust me, when the woman is found under those circumstances she was stabbed, shot to death, or beaten to a bloody pulp."

Claire tried to match Owen's matter-of-fact way of relating horrific events, but she couldn't do it. "If someone abused Maia, he must be found and punished," she said with an intensity that startled both herself and the detective.

As Owen stared back at Claire, she showed no signs of weariness in her feral and alert eyes. Claire hoped she hadn't revealed too much. It was Owen's job to know when startling truths hid behind quiet façades. She studied Claire for a while in silence, choosing her words carefully when she finally spoke. "Sure, we'd like to prosecute every man everywhere who ever abused a woman. It's difficult enough when we've got evidence, a suspect, and a victim ready, able, and willing to testify. In this case we don't have any evidence, we don't have a suspect, and the victim is dead. We don't even know who she is, and the truth is we may never know."

"What do you do with the body if you don't identify her?" Claire asked.

"Eventually it goes into a pauper's grave."

"I'll pay for the burial, if you don't locate a family."

"I'll make a note of that," Detective Owen replied.

"In all the myths I found involving the constellation Pleiades a group of boys or girls escapes into the sky. Sometimes they're siblings; sometimes they're friends. Since the constellation moves around so much it is identified with the homeless. Maybe someone molested other homeless women or Maia's sisters or girls she considered sisters." She wished she hadn't used the word "molested." The word in common usage now was "abuse." She had to remember to use the word "abuse."

"If someone . . . molested . . . Maia, it's quite possible he also abused her sisters or friends or women she never even knew," Owen said. "Sexual offenders are a lot like addicts. They tend to keep doing it until they are caught and stopped. It's important for women to speak out right away so we can catch the bastards before they do any more harm, but there are many reasons why girls keep quiet, especially in a family situation."

"If you could find Maia's identity, it might not be too late to stop the pattern."

Owen leaned back and crossed her arms. "You identify with her, don't you?" she asked.

"I have a daughter." It was as much as Claire was willing to admit.

Detective Owen stood up. "My advice is not to get obsessed with this. It's our job to ID victims and track down abusers. You need to protect the valuable books in the library."

In other words, "You do your job and I'll do mine" Claire thought, as Detective Owen left her office.

When Claire got home that evening she let the cat out and made herself a bowl of pasta for dinner. When it was good and dark and Nemesis hadn't come home yet, she went outside and found him rummaging under a rose bush. Claire looked up at the sky and saw that all the stars were in place. Somewhere above her head seven sisters wandered, pinpoints of light in the darkness, huddling together for comfort.

Claire thought about what Detective Owen had said. Abusers didn't stop until they were caught and they couldn't be caught unless a victim spoke up. She would never know how many other girls George Hogan had abused, girls who hadn't spoken out before Claire, girls who hadn't spoken out after. Had his own daughter been a victim? Claire didn't blame herself for not speaking out. She was clear about why she had kept silent. She was only twelve years old when the incident happened. But as time went by and she learned more about abuse, she began to fear she'd protected herself but left George Hogan free to molest other girls, even his own daughter. And why would George Hogan have stopped at molestation? Was that the precursor to rape? It was an issue that would bother her until she knew George Hogan was dead and in his grave.

The coyotes in the arroyo began to bark and howl. House pets weren't safe in the foothills after dark. Claire picked up her cat and took him inside.

# Chapter Seven

The next day Claire took a break after lunch and walked over to Lawton Davis's office. The UNM campus was full of sculptures, some more successful artistically than others. Claire liked the circle of stone obelisks created by a Korean artist in front of the Earth and Planetary Sciences Building where Lawton Davis worked. She knew him by reputation only as a prominent scholar in the field of archeoastronomy. She hoped his ego wouldn't turn out to be as large as his reputation but knew that was always a possibility in academia.

She found his office number in the directory, walked up a flight of stairs, and knocked on Lawton's door.

"Come in," he called.

Claire opened the door and found Lawton sitting at his desk. Instead of the usual framed awards and diplomas, the walls of his office were filled with photographs of the night skies, subtly tinted like the photographs taken by the Hubble Telescope. Lawton himself had the comfortable, rumpled look of an old sweater. His gray hair was long enough to rest on the back of his collar. His amber eyes were full of enthusiasm and light. Claire introduced herself.

"I've been wanting to meet you for a long time." He stood up and took Claire's hand in a combination squeeze and shake.

"You have?" she asked.

"Yes. I admire the work you've been doing in collection development. The university needs to continue to expand its rare-book collection."

"Thank you," Claire said. "I've heard good things about your work, too."

"Is this visit related to your work?" he asked.

"Not exactly. Have you heard about the woman who was found dead in the basement under the library?" She knew news of the death was likely to have spread all over campus by now.

"I did hear something about it," Lawton Davis replied, rubbing his chin as if feeling for a beard that was no longer there.

"The police have not been able to identify her. She left no ID. She told a student she met in the library to call her Maia."

"In Greek mythology Maia is the brightest star in the constellation Pleiades and the mother of Mercury."

"A Quentin Valor illustration from Thomas Duval's *Ancient Sites* was found in the storage room beside Maia's body. It had been carefully cut out of the Anderson Reading Room's first edition."

"Ouch." Lawton winced. "That hurts. Which illustration was it?"

"Spiral Rocks."

"Did she take anything else?"

"Not from that book."

"Odd that she would pick Spiral Rocks. All of Quentin Valor's illustrations are marvelous, of course. In my opinion he is the premier expedition artist. But if I were going to steal from a first edition of *Ancient Sites*, I would take an illustration of Chaco Canyon. It's a far more complex and interesting site. Was she planning to sell the Spiral Rocks illustration?"

"I don't know. She died of a heroin overdose. There's always the possibility she was looting valuable books and selling the illustrations for drug money or trading them for drugs."

"Was the illustration the police found in good condition?"

"Pristine," Claire said. "The razor-bladed edge was precise and perfect."

"Well," he smiled, "at least this Maia was a careful thief."

"Unfortunately I have no idea how many other books she damaged. I examined *Ancient Sites* and saw that Spiral Rocks was the only illustration taken from that book, but I can't go through every valuable illustrated book in the library."

"Of course not." Lawton shook his head in sympathy.

"Perhaps you can help."

"I'll do whatever I can."

"I talked to Maia by the duck pond last year and she pointed out the Jupiter-Venus conjunction in the evening sky."

"Everybody was talking about it. It was a marvelous event, a once-in-a-lifetime occurrence when the five naked-eyes planets came together."

"It was magnificent," Claire agreed.

"Altogether it went on for several weeks. I photographed every stage." Lawton pointed to the photographs on the walls. "When I processed the photos, I gave each of the planets a color, so the viewer could identify them as they did their slow-motion dance. Mars, as you might expect, is red. I left Venus as a golden light."

"The photographs are exquisite," Claire said, looking at the planets dancing on the wall and the approach-avoidance dynamic as Venus and Mars moved together then parted. "The colors remind me of the photographs taken by the Hubble Telescope."

"Thank you." Lawton brushed his hair away from his collar and beamed with a shy pride. Claire was touched; she saw pride often enough in academia but rarely saw anything shy about it.

"It was an absolute stroke of genius for the scientists to color the Hubble photographs," Lawton said. "It turned the pictures into artwork and made them accessible to everyone."

"Maia told me that Venus is visible in the daytime to those who know where to look," Claire said.

"That's a belief some Indians share," Lawton said.

"Considering that conversation and the fact that she was found with an illustration from *Ancient Sites*, it could be that her interest — or her drug connection's interest — was in archeoastronomy. She was homeless. I doubt she was enrolled as a student, although without knowing her name that would be hard to prove one way or the other. She may have sat in on some of your classes."

"What did she look like?"

"She wasn't someone you would especially notice. She was pale. She had good bones. Her hair was light brown. She dressed in a very neat and subdued way. The police have a photo they are showing to people who might be able to identify her. Would you be willing to take a look?"

"When was the photo taken?"

"After she died."

Lawton grimaced. "I've seen many students fall asleep in my classes," he said. "They may look like they're dead, but I'm not really keen on looking at photos of people who really are dead. If Maia sat in on a large class I wouldn't have noticed her, and she would never have been admitted to a small class."

"Maybe she talked to you at some point."

"It's possible. I talk to so many students. I can't remember everyone. Can you come up with a photograph of her alive?"

"It could be difficult," Claire said, "if not impossible."

"The impossible — now that takes a little longer." He smiled.

Claire, who felt he'd dodged the ball she'd tossed out, wondered if it was photographs of the dead he wanted to avoid or meeting with the police. She moved on to the next subject.

"Would you be able to put together a list of the library's most valuable illustrated books in the field of archeoastronomy for me? I could narrow my search for missing illustrations by starting with those books." Claire was capable of compiling such a list herself but knew Lawton Davis could do it better and faster.

"Now, that's an area in which I can help," he said. "Consider it done. In its own way Spiral Rocks is quite an interesting site. Very few people have seen it, but that should change soon. Have you ever been there?"

"No."

"It's the rare archeoastronomical site that's on private land. It was owned by a rancher in Colorado until the celestial artist Edward Girard talked him into selling it. Girard has a passion for his work that can make him a very convincing salesman. The sky is his canvas. What makes Spiral Rocks unique from an archeoastronomer's point of view is that it frames the Maximum Moon."

"What's that?" Claire asked.

"The Hopi considered the moon to be a foolish man who wanders around without a home. I'm sure you've noticed from watching the full moon rise over the Sandias that it moves north in the winter and south in the summer. Every year it reaches its southernmost point at the summer solstice and its northernmost point at the winter solstice, but those aren't fixed points. Within those extremes the moon actually has an eighteen-and-a-half-year cycle. It moves north for nine and a quarter years, then it turns south. Its northernmost and southernmost points are called the Maximum and Minimum Extremes. The Anasazi were keen observers of the night sky and they had the advantage of a sky free of ambient light. They were aware of the Maximum and Minimum Extremes. In fact, some of the buildings at Chaco are oriented toward them. The spiral on Fajada Butte has nine and a quarter turns and the Maximum and Minimum Moons cast shadows on it. In an amazing natural occurrence, the Maximum Moon rises right between Spiral Rocks every eighteen and a half years. The ancient peoples observed this and celebrated it, and so does Edward Girard. This year is a Maximum Moon year, and it will take place later this month. It's the second time that has happened since Girard bought the property. The last time he threw a large party to celebrate. He may be doing it again. He has much more to celebrate, now that he is further along in developing his observatory.

"Girard believes that isolating elements of the sky alters the viewers' perceptions. For example, we see the sky as a bowl, but if you isolate and frame a portion of it, it appears flat. The planet Venus is the third brightest light in the sky, bright enough to cast a shadow. Girard is building a chamber to isolate its light. His observatory may never be finished. He has a knack for taking on enormous projects but never completing them. Even in an incomplete stage, his observatory is an amazing achievement, one that will inspire people throughout the ages in much the same way that Chaco Canyon has. Excuse me for running on at the mouth." He laughed. "Obviously this is a project for which I have enormous enthusiasm."

"Will there be a chamber for observing Venus in the daytime?" Claire asked.

"I don't know. Offhand I would say that's not possible, but I didn't consider many of the things Edward Girard has accomplished to be possible."

"Do you know him well?"

"Not really. He's a loner and totally devoted to his work, although he can be charming when he wants to be."

"Can you tell me how I could get in touch with him? It's possible there is a connection between his observatory at Spiral Rocks and Maia. If she admired Girard's work, maybe she was planning on attending the celebration."

"Artistic men like Edward Girard have groupies and fans even when they totally ignore them," Lawton sighed. "Unlike us scholarly types."

Scholarly types had groupies, too, in Claire's experience, but Lawton Davis might be too self-effacing to be aware of that. The light in his eyes when he talked about Edward Girard's work bordered on hero worship. It was the artist's role to act out and express everything more buttoned-up types couldn't, the artist's role to be damned for his self-expression as well as to be praised for it.

"Let me see if I can find a phone number or an E-mail address," Lawton said. "Maybe I can get you an invitation to the Maximum Moon celebration."

"That would be wonderful," Claire said. She stood up. "Your photographs are beautiful. Thank you for showing them to me."

Lawton had a glow on the verge of turning into a blush, but he dimmed the light by saying, "It's nothing, really. Just a hobby.

Wait until you see Edward Girard's work. Now, there's an artist."

The next morning Lawton Davis brought his list of valuable illustrated archeoastronomy books to Claire's office. He also brought along Edward Girard's phone number and E-mail address.

"I e-mailed him about your interest," Lawton said, "but I haven't received a reply yet."

Later that afternoon Claire took the list to the Anderson Reading Room and began searching the books he'd recommended. In one sense it wasn't a difficult job; the books were works of art. To spend the afternoon sitting in a beautiful room looking at illustrations of ancient observatories, of stars, moons, planets, and constellations could hardly be considered unpleasant work. But every time she checked an index and turned to a page, Claire had the gnawing sensation she would find it missing. As she worked her way through the books, finding every illustration exactly where it was supposed to be, her *ansia* abated. Turning page after page and looking at the sky had a tranquilizing effect. By the time she'd finished Lawton's list she knew Maia hadn't been systematically looting archeoastronomy books, which made her choice of the Spiral Rocks illustration even more intriguing.

She went back to her office, called Lawton, and gave him the news.

"Excellent," he said.

Next she dialed Detective Owen's number. "Professor Lawton Davis from the Department of Earth and Planetary Sciences gave me a list of valuable archeoastronomy books," she said. "I went through all of them and found nothing else missing."

"Well, that's good news, isn't it?"

"Yes, although it's possible she had already looted books in another field and was just getting started on archeoastronomy. Or it could be that Spiral Rocks had some special meaning to Maia. Lawton Davis told me an artist named Edward Girard is turning it into an observatory and is having a celebration there in a few weeks."

"Oh?" asked Owen.

"Oh," Claire replied.

"We talked to Seth Malcolm. He admits to talking to Maia but not to giving her his code or letting her into the basement or the Anderson Reading Room."

"Do you believe him?"

"Not necessarily, although he was right about the Hope Central Shelter. We talked to Christopher Hyde, the director, who identified Maia from our photo. He said she stayed at the shelter a few years ago but started using and had to leave. She stopped using and came back last winter. She left in the spring, possibly because she had started using again. Maia kept to herself, Hyde said. She claimed she hated to be shut up indoors, but he thought she was claustrophobic. The only personal information he ever got from her was that her name was Maia and she'd used drugs."

"Have you found out who sold her the China White? Have there been any more deaths from it?"

"To both of those questions the answer is not yet. We're still investigating, but the only crimes we've found so far are the sale of the heroin and the damage to your book. No missing person's report has been filed on anyone who resembles Maia. Unfortunately heroin gets bought and sold all the time. Do books get damaged all the time?"

"I wouldn't say all the time, but more often than I'd like," Claire said. "If there are other damaged books in the library I need to know. It would help if I could further narrow my search."

"Have you thought about other expedition books? Expeditions that didn't involve archeoastronomy?"

Claire *had* thought about it. It meant making a list and going through another stack of books page by page, another day shut up in the Anderson Reading Room. But she agreed to start looking through the expedition books. Damaged books were the only legitimate involvement she had in Maia's death.

"Good luck," Detective Owen said.

Claire hung up the phone and stared at her books-with-wings screen saver. Books were her passion and her business. She was a librarian and rare-book expert. It wasn't up to her to find out who Maia was and notify the next of kin; that job belonged to the APD. To them she was just another unidentified homeless person who had OD'd, but she was the only homeless person or addict Claire had ever known. Everyone else she had encountered had a name, a history, an identity, was more than a few snippets of conversation. But it had been years since anyone had called her beautiful. Was it that compliment that connected her to Maia and drove her to find out who she was? Was it because Maia was about the same age as her own daughter and she couldn't stand the thought of Robin disappearing and dying alone in a storage room with no one to bury her or to mourn her passing? Or was it because she suspected Maia was a sister, another girl who'd longed to escape to the sky?

The books with wings flew across her computer screen — red books, green books, leather-bound books, classic books, forgotten books, boring books, illuminating books. Claire turned off the computer. She had agreed to examine the other expedition books, but she hadn't agreed to do it today. There were times when even Claire tired of books.

She called Edward Girard and got voice mail in a recorded man's voice that might, or might not, have been Edward's. She left a message saying she was interested in attending the Maximum Moon celebration and asking him to call her back as soon as possible.

# Chapter Eight

Claire left work, but instead of heading for home in the foothills she turned her truck toward the Valley. She drove west on Central, passed the cluster of movie theater, lights, restaurants, and the NYPD (the New York Pizza and Deli) that made downtown Albuquerque look almost upscale. She turned south on Third and in a few blocks she was in derelict city, the area she thought of as Mission Row, where the homeless went seeking shelter. Except for isolated pockets around Central there wasn't much street life in Albuquerque, so little that Claire sometimes questioned why the city even had sidewalks. It was a sprawling Western city where trucks and SUVs ruled. Every year people's driving-around-town vehicles got larger. In tired moments Claire thought of them as tanks that fortified and protected the drivers while giving them a sense of power that turned them belligerent. When her pickup truck was new it had seemed substantial, but now it felt like a little red wagon surrounded by a column of tanks.

Those who could protected themselves; those who couldn't walked the streets. There were people on the sidewalk in this part of town, clusters of ragtag warriors, some wearing football shirts, some wearing mini-skirts, some in camouflage. Many of the men on the street were veterans. One result of war and aggression was that even the victors ended up with no place to live. Claire passed the churches and missions that administered to the homeless and stopped at Hope Central, which displayed no cross or religious symbol. Claire had met Christopher Hyde and knew that was a deliberate choice on his part. Hope Central was a humanist shelter. The homeless came from many different walks of life and followed many different paths. Christopher's goal was to help them get back on their feet, not to convert them. The lack of a church connection made it even harder for him to raise money. Periodically he put together a book of writings and artwork created by people who had spent time at the shelter. The arts were taught at Hope Central by a loyal group of volunteers. Christopher raised money by selling this book. Claire always bought several copies for the library, but book sales rarely supported individuals, much less institutions, and Hope Central was always strapped for cash.

She parked in front of the building, which was shabby even for south Third Street. Claire had last seen Christopher Hyde at a signing the University Bookstore held for the latest edition of his book. She remembered him as a small, vibrant man with a fringe of reddish hair. Would he remember her?

Claire glanced at her watch. It was four thirty, still afternoon in her opinion. If she were at the library she would have hours of work left. But at Hope Central the day was ending. Homeless drifted toward the door like bees returning to the hive. Most of their clothes were drab and shabby. The pale, neat Maia would have stood out here. Claire negotiated her way through the swarm of people at the door, went inside, and asked a volunteer if she could speak to Christopher Hyde.

The woman gave her a quick glance, recognized that she didn't need a place for the night, and asked, "Does he know you?"

"We've met. My name is Claire Reynier. I'm a librarian at UNM."

The woman buzzed Christopher on the intercom. "Hey, Chris," she yelled, "there's a woman named Claire somethin' or other from UNM who wants to talk to you." She went back to gathering information from people at the door. "Excuse me," she said. "Dinner time."

The living room at Hope Central reminded Claire of the lobby of a seedy hotel furnished with sagging, broken-springed sofas. The room was filling with hungry people, including crying babies, squirming children, defeated and tired men with empty eyes. As the noise level escalated, she could see how the confusion and lack of privacy might have driven Maia to the sanctuary of the library.

While she waited for Christopher, Claire was drawn to the artwork on the walls of the living room, portraits of the homeless. In one way they mirrored the people in the room. Their faces showed the ravages of street life, yet their expressions were vibrant and hopeful. Many were shown as performers in an imaginary circus — clowns, tightrope walkers, animal trainers. The colors were bright as circus posters but never garish.

Christopher Hyde crossed the room, stopping several times to take a hand and smile at someone he recognized. Claire had the thought that if she were painting him, she would have painted him as a clown. His fringe of orange hair resembled a clown's ruff. His pants were baggy. He wore a yellow shirt.

Christopher took her hand. His eyes were puzzled and his forehead wrinkled in confusion. "I know we've met. I just can't remember where or when."

"I work at the Center for Southwest Research at UNM. I go to your signings at the University Bookstore. I always buy several copies of your book for the library."

"Well, that's good to know." He patted her hand and Claire saw that the back of his was ruddy and freckled. “We always need the money. Do you like our paintings?”

“They’re wonderful,” Claire said. “I love the colors, the optimism, the expressions on the subjects’ faces.”

“These are all people who stayed at the shelter at one time or another,” Christopher said. “It’s empowering for them to see themselves represented in a work of art. We sell the paintings to raise money for the shelter.” He laughed. “We’re shameless. We sell anything we can, except, of course, sex and drugs. Any drugs we confiscate are destroyed.”

“Who is the artist?”

“A woman named Lisa Teague, who teaches here. It would be hard for us to survive without the help of Lisa. I can’t walk around with my hand out all the time.”

Claire intended to make a contribution to the shelter but she hadn’t decided what to give yet. “If you have some time, I’d like to talk to you about Maia, the woman who died in the basement of Zimmerman.”

“The police told me she stole an illustration from the library.”

“I’m hoping she only stole one. Could we talk? I should have called first. I didn’t realize this would be such a busy time for you.”

“No problem. We have a half hour yet before dinner.”

He led Claire through the living room to a minuscule office in the back of the building.

The solitary window had a battered air conditioner filling the lower panes. The upper panes faced a brick wall on the far side of an alley. A bookshelf was filled with copies of Christopher's book.

"Maia was interested in art," Christopher said. "She participated in Lisa's workshops. Lisa probably knew her as well as anyone. You might want to talk to her."

"I would," Claire said.

Christopher took Lisa's card from his desk and handed it to Claire. "After all my years in this business very little shocks me, but I am surprised that Maia would steal from the library. She loved art."

"I don't know for sure that she stole it," Claire said. "I only know that an illustration was cut out of the book *Ancient Sites* and it was found in the room with Maia. It's possible she took other artwork and sold or traded it for drugs. We have so many valuable illustrated books in the library. It's difficult and time consuming to look through every one."

"*La jeringa* and the damage done," Christopher said. "Maia had a heroin addiction. I had to ask her to leave when she started using. For a while she kicked it, but she must have started up again. It's a powerful addiction, almost as powerful as cigarettes, so they say. Street life is also intoxicating. Everyone gets to be a heroine or a hero on the street. They rescue their fellow addicts by bringing them drugs or finding them a place to stay. Lisa catches some of that element of heroism-on-the-edge in her paintings, doesn't she?"

"Yes," Claire agreed.

"Life on the street is dangerous but it has a purpose. Addicts know what they have to do next to get high. That can be addicting, too. Most people kick it by going into a treatment center. Maia claimed she did it by being locked up alone in a house."

"Really?" Claire asked.

"That's what she said."

"I thought she was claustrophobic. I saw her at a reading in the Willard Reading Room. When I closed the door she panicked, pushed me aside, and ran out."

"Sometimes if a claustrophobic person has a place to see out of she can cope. A window helps, but not this window." He pointed to the brick wall and laughed a deep laugh that displayed the gold in his teeth.

"The door had a deadbolt. The maintenance man claims he locked it for the weekend, not knowing anyone was inside."

"Well, if Maia was trying to kick she wouldn't have gone into that room with heroin. An addict alone with her *ansia,* that's a recipe for disaster. What exactly was the illustration? The police didn't say."

"It was a drawing of Spiral Rocks, an

archeoastronomy site in southern Colorado that the artist Edward Girard is developing. Do you know if that place had any special meaning to her?"

"Not that I know of."

"I met her last year, and she talked to me about the Venus-Jupiter conjunction. Maia is the name of a star in the constellation Pleiades, which many cultures have considered the constellation of the homeless. It's possible she had an interest in astronomy."

"She was an intelligent woman. That was obvious. But she revealed very little else about herself while she was here."

"She told a graduate student that she became homeless because Coyote chased her."

"That's not surprising. Many women become homeless because they're running away from an abuser. They go to a new city, assume a new identity, and hope the guy won't find them. Coyote isn't a bad name for that kind of a predator."

"Do you know if Maia was an assumed name?"

"My guess would be yes, but I don't know for sure."

"I'm a mother myself. It bothers me that no one has filed a missing-person's report."

"It's tragic, isn't it," Christopher asked, "that someone as bright and attractive as Maia could fall through the cracks and no one cares?" His expression changed to the droopy frown of a clown.

"I care," Claire said.

"Good. Somebody needs to. Somebody needs to care for every single person who has ever passed through this shelter. I can't do it all myself."

"I'd like to make a contribution."

"Money is always welcome. We need sheets, we need blankets, we need pots, we need pans, we need art supplies for our workshops. You name it, we need it." He put his hand on his bookshelf. "One hundred dollars will get you a signed copy of my book. Two hundred dollars will get you two."

Claire already had signed copies of his books. "I was thinking of a painting," she said.

"The ones on the living room walls are for sale."

"They are not quite what I had in mind. Do you know if Lisa painted Maia?"

"She did. It was a lovely painting. Why don't you talk to her about it? She lives in the Old Albuquerque High School."

"I could stop by on my way home."

"I'll call her and tell her you're coming. Would you like to join us for dinner? We're having franks and beans tonight, right out of the can, and a Jell-O salad."

It sounded like the perfect comfort meal,

but Claire had other things on her mind. "I need to get going," she said. "Thanks for your help."

"My pleasure," Christopher said, smiling and squeezing her hand.

# Chapter Nine

Claire drove east on Central to the Old Albuquerque High School. For years it had been an abandoned wreck of a building with broken windows and boarded-up doors, home to derelicts and strays, but it had recently been renovated and the former classrooms turned into light-filled studios.

Claire parked her truck, went into the lobby, and rang Lisa's bell. Lisa buzzed her in. When she reached Lisa's floor, Claire found her standing in the doorway waiting. Lisa was small and slender. She wore the sandblasted jeans that were currently in fashion, but her sandblasted sections had been tinted pink instead of the usual shimmering white. Her cropped top showed her navel. Her hair was short and spiky with a purple streak. Her long fake nails were the same shade of purple. She wore rings on most of her fingers. Claire guessed her to be in her early twenties.

Lisa invited Claire into her studio, where a large window faced south looking down at Central. An easel was set up in the corner. The only paintings displayed on the walls were abstractions.

"The developers did a wonderful job with this building," Claire said.

"Didn't they?" said Lisa. "My mother rents this unit for me. It's halfway between UNM and my work at the shelter. A studio with northern light would have been better for painting, but I like looking down on Central."

"Are those your paintings?" Claire asked of the abstractions.

"No," Lisa said. "I'd never put my own work on my walls. I'd always see things I'd want to change."

"Your portraits of the homeless are wonderful," Claire said. "Christopher showed me the ones at the shelter."

Lisa seemed embarrassed by the compliment. "Chris likes to hang the paintings with circus scenes at the shelter. He loves the circus and dresses up as a clown for special events. I don't necessarily see the homeless as circus performers, but that's often how they see themselves. There's an element of fantasy in the circus that takes them away from their real lives. Everyone has a dream image. I try to find out what it is and paint that image. If I ask the homeless how they want to be portrayed, I get mumbles and blank stares or sometimes the name of a celebrity. It's better just to talk to them for a while and see where that leads. Or else I show them other portraits I've done and an idea comes out of that. Chris said you were interested in the portrait I did of Maia?"

"Yes."

Lisa squeezed her hands together. "I was shocked by her death. It seemed like she had the potential to get it together, if any of my students did. She was smarter than most of them. She came in here with a clear idea of how she wanted to be portrayed. She saw herself as dancing in a circle with other girls."

"Do you still have the painting?" Claire asked.

"No. It has been sold. Every year the Downtown Gallery on Central has an exhibit to benefit Chris's shelter. They put Maia's portrait in the window. Somebody saw it there, fell in love with it, and bought it for twenty-five hundred dollars, the best price we've ever gotten for a painting." Lisa had a proud glow and rightfully so, Claire thought.

"Do you know who bought it?" she asked.

"No. The shelter wanted to get the buyer's name, of course. A person that generous is worth keeping in touch with, but it was a cash deal and the buyer never gave the gallery a name or address."

"Someone walked in off Central with twenty-five hundred dollars in cash? Who walks around with that kind of money?" Claire asked.

"It wasn't a drug dealer, if that's what

you're thinking," Lisa said. "Even if it was, Chris probably would have sold the painting. The money all goes to a good cause. I don't get any of it. As far as my mother is concerned, I'm a grad student, not an artist."

"How do you know the buyer wasn't a dealer?" Claire asked. "Maia died of a heroin overdose. She must have gotten it from a dealer."

"The gallery owner told me the buyer was a conservatively dressed woman who said she saw the painting in the window and fell in love with it. People react strongly to my paintings."

"Of course they do. You do exceptional work."

"Thank you." Lisa turned away from the compliment and walked across the room to her computer. "I photograph all my paintings and store the images on my computer. Would you like to see Maia's?"

"I would."

Lisa tapped a few keys and brought up an image of girls in long white dresses dancing in a circle. Most of their faces were turned away, hidden by swirling hair or blurred in the motion of the dance. But one face was perfectly clear — Maia as she might have appeared in her early teens or even younger. She had the same high cheekbones and brown hair but this face had vitality, youthful optimism, and color.

"It's lovely," Claire said.

"I call it *Summertime*. That's Maia, of course," Lisa said. "Maybe you noticed that there is only one clear face in each of my paintings. I like to give the homeless a moment in the sun, one moment they don't have to share with anyone else. It makes them feel important, if only for a little while."

"Did Maia say how many girls she wanted in the painting?"

"She wanted a total of seven."

"Did she tell you how old she wanted to be?"

"Twelve. I had to imagine what Maia would have looked like at twelve. She seemed to think I got it right."

Lisa's computer had a large screen with high resolution. Claire could clearly see New Mexico in the background of the painting. "The adobe wall, the mountains in the background, the hollyhocks in bloom — were those her idea?"

"Not exactly. She wanted a New Mexican setting and that was my interpretation."

"Did that make you think that she was raised in New Mexico?"

"Maybe, or maybe she wished she'd been raised here. I couldn't say."

"If she was raised in New Mexico, a mother or someone here should be looking for her. According to the APD no one has filed a missing-person's report."

"People from a happy home don't run away and live on the street," Lisa said. She had a youthful style, but her work had given her a wise and mature outlook. "Most of them want nothing to do with the people they left behind. Often they are afraid they will be pursued. It's unusual for them to choose an image of themselves as younger or as part of a family. They prefer to be painted as part of the circus, or alone, or with animals. I don't know if these girls were Maia's real sisters or friends or just people she imagined."

"Was Maia her real name?" Claire asked.

"I doubt it. Most of the people I meet don't use their real names."

Claire stared at the seven girls dancing on the screen. There was a shadow in the corner cast by a tree outside the frame of the painting that seemed to be reaching towards the girls. "In Greek mythology Maia is one of the seven daughters of Atlas and Pleione," Claire said. "They were playing in the woods when Orion, the hunter, saw them and became infatuated. He pursued the girls but Zeus saw the sisters were in danger and he turned them into doves who flew away into the sky. They became the constellation Pleiades."

"I didn't know that," Lisa said, "but it wouldn't surprise me if Maia identified with that story. What homeless person wouldn't rather be a star in the sky?"

"Do you know if she had an interest in astronomy?"

"She never talked about it to me. Maia was very intelligent, but shy. She didn't like to talk about herself. Mostly we talked about Chris, the other people at the shelter, how she spent her days studying in libraries around town, visiting museums, attending public lectures and readings. I was glad I was able to paint her dancing and happy as she might have been. Did you know her well?"

"Not really. I talked to her twice, but I wouldn't say I knew her. I got involved because the police found an illustration stolen from the library in the storage room with Maia's body. It was Spiral Rocks, an ancient site in southern Colorado. Did she ever say anything about Spiral Rocks to you?"

Lisa shook her head. "No. Chris said she died from a heroin overdose. She seemed straight when I saw her, but it doesn't surprise me that she would get on drugs. Many people at Hope Central get there because they abused drugs. Some of them even ask me to paint them the way they feel when they are high. Look at this." Lisa's long nails clicked a few keys and another image filled the screen. "This woman was a friend of Maia's. It's a tough painting that has been hard to sell."

A woman with hair streaked the color of cherry Jell-O floated above a river. She had a stoned expression with a smile full of holes. Her body stretched out like smoke as it followed the curves of the river.

"That looks like Ansia," Claire said.

"You know her?"

"Zimmerman Library is a mecca for the homeless," Claire said. "Sometimes Ansia hangs out there. She and Maia were friends?"

"Yes. They looked out for each other. Would you like me to print out a copy of Maia's image for you?"

"Please. Could I have Ansia's, too?"

"No problem."

When the images were printed Lisa apologized for the poor quality, but Claire got what she wanted — a face recognizable as an alive and vibrant Maia. "Did you paint her in this room?" she asked.

"Yes. I do all my portraits of the homeless here. It's convenient for me and for them."

"Did Maia seem claustrophobic to you?"

"She might have been. She asked me to leave the door open. She sat at the window."

"I'm afraid she panicked when the maintenance man locked the door to the storage room and that's why she took the heroin."

"Any addict who has heroin in her possession is going to use it," Lisa said. "Maia might have already been high when she went into the basement."

It was a possibility Claire hadn't considered. She studied the portraits Lisa had given her. Even in the form of color printouts from a computer, they were exceptional. "Are you in the School of Fine Arts at the university?" she asked.

"No. I'm getting a master's in social work."

"You're very talented. I hope you'll continue painting. Many people can do social work, but very few are artists."

"I'd like to paint," Lisa said, twisting her rings around on her fingers. "But I made a promise to my mom that if she helped me get through school, I'd find a real job. She raised me herself. It was often a struggle for her. She'd like me to have some security in my life."

Lisa's talent was her security, Claire thought, but she wasn't Lisa's mom. She thanked Lisa for her help and left her studio.

# Chapter Ten

Before she headed home, Claire turned her truck around and drove west again on Central. By now it was dinner time for most people and a line had formed at Tucanos Brazilian Grill. Other Central Avenue businesses stayed open later now that the movie theater and Tucanos brought people downtown in the evening. Claire drove a few blocks farther, parked, and walked to the Downtown Gallery. Most of the people downtown were clustered around the theaters, bars, and restaurants. The block the gallery was on was quiet enough that Claire wouldn't want to hear the sound of footsteps behind her. Lights were on at the Downtown Gallery. The windows were full of Southwestern scenes — clouds billowing in blue skies, piñones casting long shadows — scenes Claire had seen often enough in life and in art. The paintings in these windows were too ordinary to have pulled her into the gallery.

She opened the door and stepped inside. A tinkling bell alerted a woman who sat at a table leafing through a magazine. Emotions ruffled the woman's face before she spoke: annoyance that she had been interrupted, alarm that someone had entered the gallery at this hour, then relief that Claire didn't appear to be a threat and might even be a legitimate customer.

"Hello," the woman said, standing up to greet Claire. "How are you?"

She wore a plum-colored dress with a stained-glass pendant hanging from her neck. Her hair was blond and silky as a spaniel's. It rested on her shoulders but she cupped her hand and pushed it up as if she was afraid it was going to fall out. Her voice was bright and quick. Her manner was nervous.

Claire found herself mimicking the woman's chirpy tone as she replied, "I'm fine. And you?"

"Good. It has been quiet tonight."

"Do you always stay open in the evening?" Claire asked.

"After Tucanos opened, Rachel, the owner, thought it would be a good idea, but we don't get many customers at night. I'm Linda Butler." She extended her hand.

"Claire Reynier."

"People are willing to come downtown at night to eat or go to the movies but not to buy art. Not yet, anyway. Rachel wanted to stay open until nine, but I talked her into closing at eight." She looked at her watch. "Only half an hour to go. Do you like Janelle Alarid's work?" Linda asked, waving her hand at the Southwest landscapes. "She has an elegant style, don't you think?"

Claire thought that was more a statement of hope than of fact. To her the paintings lacked any style. "Actually I was interested in the Hope Central show," she said.

"That show closed. The artist, Lisa Teague, does incredible work. The gallery is always busy when the Hope Central show is on, although a lot of the traffic is homeless people looking at pictures of themselves and their friends. It's a good cause. We take a tiny commission, but most of the money goes to Hope Central. The show usually sells out."

"I work at Zimmerman Library at UNM," Claire said. "A homeless woman I met there was in one of Lisa's paintings called *Summertime*. She told me you sold it."

"That was a gorgeous painting," Linda said. "Absolutely gorgeous. Rachel put a high price on it, twenty-five hundred dollars, but it was worth every penny. We had it in the window for two weeks. There were a lot of inquiries but no one willing to pay the price. Usually Lisa's paintings go for around a thousand. The last night of the show a woman came in and said she had to have it and that was that."

"Did you get the woman's name, by any chance?"

Linda tugged her pendant as she asked, "Why do you want to know?"

"The homeless woman in the painting was

found dead recently in a storage room under the library. The police haven't been able to identify her and notify the next of kin. They've been showing a photograph taken after her death around the library. People will glance at a photo of a dead person, but they won't really look at it. I thought if I had an image of her alive it would help to identify the victim. If I could find the owner of the painting she could give me a photo of it. She might even know the woman's identity." It sounded convincing enough to Claire, especially since she hadn't mentioned that she already had a copy of the painting in her truck. Linda seemed too preoccupied with closing time to scrutinize Claire's words. Her eyes kept turning toward the door as if measuring the degree of darkness beyond the glass.

"Usually we do get buyers' names and addresses," she said. "Especially when we're selling for Hope Central, because Chris likes to put the names on his donors' list and hit them up again. The woman who bought *Summertime* paid cash. I didn't get her name."

"Twenty-five hundred dollars is a lot of cash to have on Central, isn't it?" Claire said. "Who carries around that kind of money?"

"She wasn't a hooker or a drug dealer, if that's what you're thinking." Linda took a good look at Claire. "She was a normal woman like you and me. She wore jeans, casual but neat. She was about our age, old enough not to feel comfortable walking around Central alone at night."

Claire had placed Linda in her midforties. The gallery light, which focused on the paintings rather than the customers, was flattering. It was possible Linda judged Claire to be younger than she actually was.

As she filled the room with her chatter, Linda reminded Claire of moths beating their wings against the light. "It's the kids who like to come down here after dark and they don't buy art. I keep telling Rachel that, but after we made twenty-five hundred dollars on the *Summertime* sale she thought it would happen again. Most of the time I sit here all by myself or I'm trying to get rid of the street people who wander in. The woman told me she was visiting from out of town and didn't like to carry her credit cards when she was on Central. I said we would hold the painting and she could come back for it the next day. But she had to leave early in the morning, she said, and she wanted to take it home with her. She went to get the money from an ATM machine or the friend she was traveling with, I'm not sure which. I promised to keep the gallery open for another hour. She came back with twenty-dollar bills. She took the painting. I put the money in the safe. That was that."

"When was it?" Claire asked.

"Let me see. It was the last night of the show. That would have been the Thursday before Memorial Day. The next day we set up the Janelle Alarid show and it opened on Saturday."

"Can you tell me any more about the woman's appearance? Her height? The color of her hair? Was there anything to distinguish her?"

Linda shrugged. "She was average height. She wore a hat so I couldn't tell what color her hair was. Really, there was nothing about her you would especially remember." She glanced at her watch, cupped her hair in her hand and pushed it higher. "Anything else? It's eight o'clock. Rachel told me to close at eight. I'm ready to go home."

"Did the homeless woman in *Summertime* ever come into the galley?"

"Not that I noticed."

"Thanks for your help," Claire said.

"Where did you park?" Linda asked her.

"In the next block."

"I park right behind the gallery myself. I'll watch you walk to your car."

It seemed excessively cautious to Claire; it was only eight o'clock. But she agreed.

"Night seems to come earlier every year," Linda said as Claire left the gallery.

She stood in the doorway and watched Claire walk to her truck. The back light from the gallery turned her into a solitary silhouette. The street was empty except for a bunch of kids pushing and shoving each other farther down Central near the El Rey Theatre. What did Linda intend to do if something happened? Claire wondered. If someone grabbed her purse, what could she do but call the police? By the time they arrived whatever could have happened would have.

Claire opened the door of her truck and climbed in. She turned toward the gallery and watched while Linda shut the door, hung a closed sign in the window, and turned off the light. She knew what Linda meant when she said night seemed to come earlier every year. It was easy to fall into the habit of staying home after dark and going to bed early. On the surface other parts of town might appear safer than Central, but the truth was life was dangerous no matter where you lived. Claire thought it was better to remember that fact than to pretend otherwise, but to creep around like a scared rabbit was a sure way to attract the predators.

She turned her truck around and drove east on Central in the direction of UNM and home. There was still a line waiting to get into Tucanos. She stopped at the light and thought about the woman who bought the painting, the woman Linda claimed was uncomfortable on Central. Did that mean she was from a small town? Linda said she was approximately their age. But Claire judged Linda to be several years younger, which could place the woman anywhere in her forties or fifties. She wore a hat that covered her hair, and jeans. That didn't reveal much; everybody wore jeans. The maximum amount Claire could get from her own ATM machine was five hundred dollars. With that limitation the woman would have had to hit every ATM downtown to come up with twenty-five hundred dollars cash, unless she got some or all of it from the friend.

Claire had a number of questions. Was the friend a man or a woman? Why would the friend be carrying around twenty-five hundred dollars in twenty-dollar bills? ATM yuppie money was also street money, drug money, the price of a BB. Middle-aged women abused drugs, too, but they preferred prescription drugs. The people who used street drugs like crack or heroin rarely made it to middle age. The woman bought the painting on Thursday evening. Maia died over the weekend. If a man had bought the painting, Claire would have suspected him of being Coyote. But a woman the right age to be Maia's mother? Why did that woman have to have the painting immediately? Maybe the woman fell in love with it and it was as simple as that. Maybe the painting reminded the woman of her own youth or her own daughter. Or maybe she recognized Maia. Claire drifted into the realm of fantasy with this thought, a place far removed from the lights on Central but not so far away from the atmosphere in Lisa Teague's studio. It was a fantasy that somehow Maia and her mother would reconnect. Claire recognized the face in the painting as the young Maia, but it had only been a few weeks since she had seen her. Would someone who hadn't seen her for years recognize her face? Someone who knew her when she was younger might. Besides, there was another clue in the painting — the seven girls dancing in a circle. Anyone who knew the myth of Maia would know what that meant. So might someone who knew the reality.

Claire continued east on Central, wondering whether Maia had seen her own portrait in the window of the Downtown Gallery. If she had, would the exposure have empowered her or terrified her into hiding in the basement of Zimmerman with her stolen illustration and her drugs?

# Chapter Eleven

Around the university Central was as busy as it was near Tucanos. Claire parked her truck at Kinko's. She could have made copies of *Summertime* at CSWR but it meant circling around the university to the lot behind Zimmerman. Kinko's was far more convenient. She went inside and ordered ten color copies. When they were done, she turned them over and wrote her own name and number on the back. Her excuse for not writing Detective Owen's number was she didn't happen to have it with her. As she wrote down her own name and number Claire felt she was stepping out of her comfort zone and dancing at the edge of her circle.

She left Kinko's and walked down Central, not knowing exactly where she was going or what she was going to do when she got there. If she came across Ansia, she would ask her about Maia, but she didn't see Ansia or anyone else dressed like a street person. Everyone she passed looked like a student or a professor or a wanna-be lugging a backpack and talking on a cell phone. Then Claire turned down Yale and saw the poet shuffling toward her. He was a tall, shaggy man who wore several layers of clothes even in the middle of summer, another homeless habitué of the library. Students jokingly called him Ralph Waldo Emerson, and somehow he had adopted the name of Waldo. Claire had spoken to him before in the library and found him to be confused but polite.

She stopped him and said, "Waldo, I'm Claire Reynier. Do you remember me from the library?"

"Evening, ma'am," Waldo said, bobbing his head and giving the impression that if he wore a hat he would be tipping it.

"I'm looking for Ansia. Do you know her?"

"Sure. I know her." He bent over to whisper. "She pees on her clothes." He held his nose. "She says the smell keeps the coyotes away."

"Would you tell her I'm looking for her?"

Waldo shuffled his feet and nodded again.

Claire took that as a yes and handed him a photocopy of *Summertime*. "That's my name and number on the back. Ansia can call me anytime. Do you recognize Maia, the girl in the picture?"

"Tiny dancer," Waldo said. "I remember her."

"She died a few weeks ago in a storage room under the library."

"I heard that," Waldo said. "It's hard to get under the library nowadays. You have to know someone who will let you in. Did Lisa paint this picture?"

"Yes."

"She painted me once when I lived in the shelter, but now I'm a street person. Lisa can't paint me anymore. Chris Hyde says you have to be homeless to have your picture painted, but what he really means is you have to be staying in his shelter."

"How did Lisa paint you?" Claire asked.

Waldo seemed startled. "As a poet. I am a poet. Ansia pretends to be a poet, but I am a real, true, honest-to-goodness poet." He pulled a poem out of his backpack and handed it to Claire. "That's my name and number on the back." He flipped the poem over, showing the back of it to be totally blank. He laughed. "No name, no number, no permanent address. I gotta go. If I see Ansia, I'll tell her you're looking." He tipped his imaginary hat, did a shuffling little two-step and ambled down the street.

That had been enough encounters for one evening and Claire was more than ready to go home. She drove across town to the Heights and turned down her street, glad she had a house, a bed, and a cat waiting at the door. He wove a path between her legs while she walked to the kitchen and opened a can of cat food. The homeless at Hope Central had eaten franks and beans for dinner, probably from industrial-sized cans. Claire hadn't eaten franks and beans since she was a kid on Hawley Lake, but it was a meal she used to serve her father when her mother wasn't home. She opened the door of her cupboard and stared at the shelves. No franks and beans, no Jell-O, no comfort food. She found a box of penne and a can of white beans. She made pasta with fagioli, spicing it with black olives and pimentos. After she cleaned the kitchen, she took the copies of the paintings and Waldo's poem into her living room and sat down on the sofa. The poem was handwritten in pencil on a sheet of white paper.

*Early to bed and early to rise*
*9-5 was just a disguise*
*I thought of all the things I could do*
*And I signed up for the poetry crew*
*Wrote all day and wrote all night*
*One day my words they really took fright*

Had Waldo meant "fright" or "flight"? He could be incomprehensible in person, but his handwriting was perfectly legible. Claire decided he had said what he meant — "fright." A blank sheet of paper could open the door to many fears.

She stared at the photocopy of *Summertime*. Seven girls danced in white summer dresses while a shadow closed in on them. Then she looked at Ansia floating above the river in a stoned state of mind where there was no fear.

Claire got up and filled the bathtub with hot water and lavender bath oil. She pinned up her hair and climbed in, sinking down until the water reached her chin. While she soaked, she thought about fear, pondering which was worse — the fear caused by other people or the fear created by your own mind. For her, agoraphobia had been worse than reality, but she had been touched by a family friend. She hadn't been raped. She hadn't been beaten. She hadn't been victimized by a family member year after year after year. The assault on her body had been brief. She was able to get away, run home to her parents, her dog, her bed, but an animal was conceived during that attack, a rodent with sharp little teeth that lived inside her and gnawed at her nerves.

She'd learned that the rodent was aroused by anxiety and hunger, stimulated by sugar, calmed by routine. It remained dormant if she shut down her senses and focused on her will. Battling her phobia gave her life heroism and purpose just like the lives of the people who lived on the street. She became a teenage warrior, but by the time she went to the U of A she had the phobia under control.

Leaving her comfort zone and going to Europe with her girlfriends was a victory, but she lost a battle in Venice at the edge of Piazza San Marco. She had left her friends and spent the winter semester traveling with Pietro Antonelli, an Italian student she met in Spain. They traveled through Morocco in his Volkswagen van that broke down in every country they visited. Then they made their way north through Spain and France into Italy, where Claire had to make the overwhelming decision whether to return to school and family in Arizona or to stay in Italy with Pietro. They'd had a fight and were on the verge of a bitter breakup. She hadn't been eating or sleeping.

She stood at the edge of the open space, thinking she would lose her mind if she stepped into it. The threat of insanity filled Piazza San Marco. Tourists scattered bread crumbs and gangs of pigeons swooped down and snatched them up. Rodents were gathering around the edges of the piazza, rats that could chew her mind to shreds. You're being stupid, she said to herself. It's not the piazza or Pietro you're afraid of, it's yourself. You're afraid of growing up, you're afraid of being a woman. She wanted to run but she made herself turn slowly away from the piazza and walk back to the hotel room. She got into bed and pulled the covers up to her chin. Although it was ninety degrees, she was shivering.

When Pietro returned to the room, they

made love with a sad tenderness. Afterward she snuggled beside him and told him the story of George Hogan's betrayal and the fear she thought she had conquered.

"Is that why you have to go home?" he asked her.

"It's just that staying in Italy is too big a step for me right now."

"I am sorry that man touched you, Clara," Pietro said, kissing the top of her head. "But it doesn't matter to me. I love you. You're not alone in the world. The same thing has happened to other girls I know."

"Really?" Claire asked.

"Sure. It's always an uncle or a family friend, so the girls don't want anybody to know. But keeping it hidden is poison."

For years Claire had felt isolated by George Hogan's hands, but Pietro told her she had sisters in other parts of the world. Now she knew there were girls in the sky, as well.

Claire sat up, flipped open the drain, and listened to the water gurgling out of the tub. Girls who'd been abused didn't wear a badge. Anxiety was one obvious clue. So were homelessness and drugs. Claire's buttoned-up attitude was more subtle, but Maia might have seen something that made her think she had a sister.

Claire stepped out of the bath and reached for a towel. A handful of moths flew out, flapping their wings in her face. She shouldn't be surprised by moths anymore, but they still startled her.

In the middle of the night she heard the sound of a girl crying. Her father came into her bedroom and sat down on the edge of her bed.

"You were crying," he said. "Are you all right?"

"No."

"Are you afraid?"

"Yes."

"Of what?"

"Everything."

"I have fears, too," he confided. "I can't stand to be closed in. I'm afraid of tunnels. I don't even like to be in movie theaters."

She knew that.

"I'm afraid I've passed my fears on to you."

"It's not your fault."

He had come to her room to comfort her, to tell her everyone had problems, even fathers, and she shouldn't be ashamed of or embarrassed by hers. She loved her father, but it didn't comfort her to know that he had fears. It was her chance to tell him about George Hogan, but she couldn't do it. She felt that her father was even more vulnerable than she was. She never told anyone about George Hogan until the night in

Venice when she told Pietro. She would always be grateful to him for listening.

Not long ago she had tracked him down in Florence, where he now taught, and contacted him by E-mail. When he told her that he was married and his wife was dying of cancer, she felt it was wrong to go on fantasizing about him. There hadn't been any E-mails for months. But she saw now that there was a reason to be in touch that went deeper than dreams and memories of romance. Pietro had opened doors and helped her by listening and telling her she wasn't alone. Now it was her turn to be there for him.

In the morning she typed an E-mail that was brief but full of feeling, a poem in spirit if not in style. By now everybody their age knew death and fear. She couldn't say to him that I am the only one who knows what you are going through, but she could say

> Pietro, something happened recently that reminded me of how valuable you were to me when you listened to my story in Venice. You changed my perception of myself, and I will always be grateful to you for that. I know what a difficult time this must be for you. If you need me, remember that I am here.

Now that she had finished it, she didn't know how to end it. She tried variations on the theme of "best": "all my best," "best wishes," "best regards." None of the "bests" seemed right. She moved on to "yours:" "yours always," "forever yours." They weren't right, either. "Cheers?" "Onward?" They were words she used for friends, not former lovers. She settled on "fondly" and clicked the SEND button.

# Chapter Twelve

When she got to work in the morning Claire took a couple of thumbtacks and pinned *Summertime* to her wall in a place where it could easily be seen from her desk. Unlike Celia's office where every surface was covered with weavings, paintings, sculptures, santos, and *milagros,* Claire's still had plenty of white space to fill. Claire sat down at her desk and studied the placement of the picture. She got up to straighten it, then called Celia.

"Can you come to my office? There's something I want to show you."

"Okay."

Celia came to the doorway wearing a beige linen dress and a necklace with matching bracelet made of spikes of coral. She spotted the *Summertime* addition immediately. "That's it?"

"Yes," Claire said.

"Where did it come from?"

"An artist named Lisa Teague paints the homeless at the Hope Central Shelter. The paintings are sold to raise money. You saw the photo of the dead Maia. Could you identify her here?"

"That's easy. Only one of the girls is

showing her face. It has to be Maia, no?" Celia walked up close to examine the picture.

"Yes. That's how she asked to be painted, the way she looked when she was twelve years old, dancing in a circle with six other girls. Lisa made me a copy. The painting has been sold."

"Do you think that someone who only knew the adult Maia could identify her in this painting?"

"It's possible," Claire said. "She looks much brighter, livelier, and younger here, but the bone structure and the hair are the same. The Downtown Gallery had an exhibit of Lisa's paintings and this one was in the window. A woman walked in off the street and paid twenty-five hundred dollars cash the Thursday before Memorial Day. It makes me wonder if she knew Maia and recognized her. If she knew the story of the seven sisters."

"You'd better tell that to Detective Owen. We need to find out who Maia was and who let her into the basement. Harrison has been on my case about it. In his opinion it's my fault that she got into the storage room."

"That's not fair. You have to give a code to everyone who works and studies here. It's not your job to police the department."

"You know as well as I do that Harrison is not fair. He has too much tenure, too much seniority, and far too much ego to be fair."

"True."

"It's a beautiful picture," Celia said. "It looks good in here."

She left the office without saying, "It's about time you put some artwork on your wall," but Claire suspected she was thinking it.

Claire sent Lawton Davis an E-mail telling him she had a picture of Maia she wanted to show him. Then she went to the Anderson Reading Room and began to search the illustrated expedition books. With trepidation she opened *Incidents of Travel in Central America, Chiapas and Yucatan* by John Lloyd Stephens with illustrations by Frederick Catherwood. It was a book she dearly loved. It was a good omen that every one of Catherwood's classic drawings of the Mayan ruins was in place. As she went though the Stephen Long expedition illustrations by Titian Ramsay Peale and the *Journals of the Wilkes Expedition* and found every illustration exactly where it was supposed to be, her anxiety began to fade. The deeper she got into the task, the more she could enjoy the beauty of the expedition illustrations. By late afternoon when the last book had been put back in its place on the shelf still intact, she was close to believing that Maia had not been systematically looting the library and trading the illustrations for drugs, that there had to have been another reason for taking Spiral Rocks.

She went back to her office and called Detective Owen, watching the girls dance across her wall while she dialed the number.

"And how are you?" Detective Owen asked.

"Good. And you?"

"Busy," Detective Owen said. Claire had heard on the news about a murder-suicide in the South Valley and wondered if Owen was involved in the investigation.

"I won't take up much of your time," she said. "I went through all the expedition books today, and I didn't find a single missing illustration."

"Good," Owen said.

"It could be that Maia had a reason to take Spiral Rocks, and that's the only illustration she took." Claire told Owen about Lisa Teague and *Summertime* and asked if she would like to come by to see her copy of the painting.

"I won't be able to do it today," Owen said. "Could you fax me a copy?"

"Sure," Claire said. "The original of the painting was in the window of the Downtown Gallery in a show of Lisa Teague's paintings to benefit the Hope Central Shelter. Linda Butler, who works at the gallery, told me that a woman saw the painting in the window, said she had to have it, and paid twenty-five hundred dollars cash."

"When was that?"

"The Thursday before Memorial Day."

"We'll check it out," Detective Owen said.

"Thanks for your help."

Claire faxed the picture to Owen. Then she tried Edward Girard's number again and was surprised when a woman answered.

"I'm Jennifer Rule, Edward Girard's publicist," the woman said. "Can I help?" She had a rapid-fire, I-have-too-much-to-do way of speaking as if she had about thirty seconds for Claire.

"I'm interested in Edward Girard's work," Claire said. "I'd like to come to the Spiral Rocks opening."

"Come, then," Jennifer replied. "It's this Saturday. Everyone's welcome. Be sure you get here before sunset in time to watch the moon rise. We have a place to camp on the property. Bring your sleeping bag if you want to spend the night."

After Claire hung up, she sat looking at her books-with-wings screen saver and thinking about who she could ask to accompany her. Celia was her first choice, but she knew Celia and her husband had plans to go to a wedding in California this weekend. She tried her friend the bookseller, John Harlan.

"Damn," he said. "I'd love to go, but I have to work."

She called her friend Madeline in Tucson, who also had plans. It was one of the rare occasions when Claire wished she still had a husband, a companion who'd accompany her to every movie she wanted to see and drop whatever he was doing for a quick trip to Spiral Rocks. But she reminded herself that when she did have a husband, he wasn't that companion. She and Evan never took spur-of-the-moment trips anywhere. Every excursion was mapped out and planned in advance. Even the music they played in the car was chosen by Evan. Whenever they went to the movies it was a movie he wanted to see.

There was a knock at the door and she looked up to see Lawton Davis's shy smile. "Am I interrupting?" he asked. "You look like you're deep in thought."

"Come in. I just got an invitation from Edward Girard's publicist to the opening at Spiral Rocks. I'm debating whether to go."

"Of course you should go," Lawton said. "It's a once-in-a-lifetime opportunity. When is it?"

"Saturday night." Claire hesitated, then said, "The invitation wasn't just for me. Anybody can go. Girard's publicist said, Everyone's welcome.' " The thought that Lawton Davis would be a fun companion was rising to the surface. He knew so much about astronomy. His enthusiasm made him a pleasure to be with.

He sighed. "Unfortunately I can't do it. I have family commitments this weekend, but you must go and tell me all about it. Promise?"

"Promise," Claire said.

"Is that the picture of Maia?" He looked at the wall.

"Yes." Claire gave him one of the copies she'd made. "A woman named Lisa Teague paints the homeless for the Hope Central Shelter. The Downtown Gallery sells the paintings and the money goes to the shelter. This is a copy of a portrait Lisa painted of Maia."

"It's lovely," Lawton said. "I'm sure you noticed that the seven girls dancing mirror the seven stars in Pleiades."

"Maia asked to be painted that way, but she didn't tell Lisa why. We don't know for sure that she was familiar with the myth."

Lawton studied the image. "Of course she was. The name is more than a coincidence."

"Do you recognize her?"

"She looks very young in this picture, younger than anyone I would have in a class unless she was a child prodigy. Child prodigies I remember."

"She wanted to be painted as she looked when she was twelve years old."

"Even if I try to age her mentally by several years I do not remember this woman." Lawton turned away from the picture and focused on Claire. "So it's up to you to go to Spiral Rocks or wherever necessary to find out who she is and why she died with that illustration by her side."

"Well, actually, it's up to the police," Claire corrected him.

"Ah, but are they willing to go all the way to Spiral Rocks? Besides, they don't have the resources of the University at their disposal and you do. They haven't even been to see *me* yet."

"I gave Detective Owen your name. The police department has murders to solve. For them Maia is just another unidentified overdose."

"But not for you."

"Not for me," Claire agreed. "I've gone through all the illustrated expedition books now, plus all the astronomy books. The only missing illustration I've found is Spiral Rocks."

"Then you must go. The experience will be unforgettable. And when you get back, tell me all about it."

"I will," Claire promised.

Lawton had given Claire a mandate. Considering the importance of the occasion, she knew she had to go. Her truck had a camper shell. She could sleep in it if she stayed too late to drive to the nearest motel. Since Spiral Rocks was in a remote corner of southern Colorado, the nearest motel could be fifty miles away. Claire debated what one wore to the opening of a celestial artist's archeoastronomical site. Jeans would be comfortable for the drive, especially her favorite Levi's 501s, but something fancier might be better for the festivities. An outdoor, full moon celebration was likely to bring out the sixties in people — if there was any sixties left in people. Her daughter, Robin, used to wear Claire's sixties clothes to costume parties, but since Robin had grown up those clothes had vanished. They might even be walking down the street on the back of a homeless person. They were unlikely to fit anymore, anyway — the sixties were Claire's skinny days. She went to her closet and picked out a long skirt and a crocheted top.

Claire hated to go to parties alone, especially parties where she didn't know anyone. To start a conversation with a stranger at a party was about as comfortable as stripping naked. But this event would be different. She was unlikely to know anyone but she had a purpose beyond networking and chitchat. She could wander around the site, look at the observation chambers, and watch the moon rise without having to make conversation. The only person she really had to talk to was Edward Girard. It could be difficult to get him alone long enough to ask if he knew Maia. She planned to bring along her copy of *Ancient Sites* with the Quentin Valor illustration as well as a photocopy of *Summertime*. Lisa's painting was a good way to start a conversation. Claire didn't have a copy of the police photo, but even if she did a photo of a dead person was less likely to start a conversation than to bring it to an end.

# Chapter Thirteen

Claire took the brand-new Highway 550 through Cuba. When the route became a four-lane highway, it was assigned a new number, but Claire remembered the old Route 44, especially the days when it was under construction and a white-knuckle drive all the way to Farmington. Traffic was let through the only open lane one direction at a time. If anyone ignored the signal to stop, a head-on collision was almost inevitable. Drivers sped up and passed on all the blind curves and places marked with no-passing signs. It was promised that the new road would be worth the expense and make driving a pleasure, and eventually it did. Claire enjoyed the drive through the red rock canyons and the wide open spaces. There were many places in the Southwest where eons of wind and water had whipped the rock into the shapes of sentinels.

Claire crossed into Colorado feeling she lived in a middle zone between the poverty of the third world and the affluence of the first. In a sense New Mexico had two foreign borders — Mexico and Colorado. The houses were more spectacular in Colorado. Vacation homes of several thousand square feet sprawled across hillsides in inaccessible places. Even the SUVs seemed bigger. The people looked taller and blonder. But the roads were no better. The dirt road that led into Spiral Rocks was as tortuous as many in New Mexico. It had almost enough ruts and bumps to make Claire wish she owned an SUV, although she had sworn to herself that she would never buy one. There were times when the rattle of her camper shell made it sound like it was about to fall off.

She could see the spiral rocks silhouetted against the sky for miles before she reached them. They were distinguished from other pinnacle rocks because they sat on top of a mesa with no other formations nearby.

By the time her truck had climbed the serpentine road up the mesa it was late afternoon and a large crowd had gathered. Claire saw people of all ages, from infants to elders, dressed in expensive hiking gear, faded jeans, or the bright embroidery of Santa Fe ethnic, which made those New Mexicans seem like poor artistic second cousins who had to dress flamboyantly to be noticed. The vehicles were mostly SUVs and trucks.

Claire followed the arrows to the section designated campground, found a place, and parked. Other visitors were busy setting up their tents. Claire stayed in her jeans but changed into the crocheted top and put on her hiking boots before walking across the mesa.

The isolated area was as flat as a tabletop and a perfect location for viewing the sky. No towns could be seen. There was little artificial light, no plumes of smoke from power plants, no pollution, nothing between the mesa and the sky. Claire saw a weathered wooden house on the northern side of the mesa. The twin spires were located on the eastern edge. Over the millennia they had been twisted into pink-and-beige spindle shapes by wind and water. The emptiness between them was filled once every eighteen and a half years by the rising of the Maximum Moon. It would be a major disappointment, Claire thought, if it happened on an overcast night. Tonight, however, the sky was perfectly clear.

As she walked she blended into a crowd moving toward the rocks. Excitement moved through the gathering like wind rustling dry leaves.

"I was here the last time," Claire heard a man behind her say. "That was before any of the chambers were built."

"I was only two years old then," his younger companion replied.

"It was spectacular," the older man said. "The moon came over the top of the mesa roaring like a lion."

Claire was glad the crowd was large

enough for her to disappear inside it. She had wondered what Edward Girard looked like and how she would identify him, but that turned out to be easy; he was surrounded by admirers. When the crowd parted Claire saw him standing near the rocks. He had a strong, muscular upper body on top of long, thin legs. His dark brown hair was thick and shoulder length. His face was radiant when he smiled but seemed gaunt and haunted in repose. Edward Girard acted like he was tolerating the admiration rather than enjoying it. Claire's impression was that whatever he had created here, he'd created it for himself. The audience was only the means to an end, the support and money that enabled him to build his monument. Edward was the center of this crowd, but he was almost as alone in it as she was.

She turned away from the rocks and began to explore the monument, waiting for a better time to talk to Edward. The spiral rocks reaching for the sky were the centerpiece, but the artist couldn't take any credit for creating them. He could take credit for the buildings, however. Unlike the massive pyramids constructed by the ancients, Edward had built a series of small, round chambers, spread out across the mesa like cups turned upside down or inverted caves cut out of cliffs. They had the rough exterior finish of rock.

Claire followed the crowd as it drifted in and out of the chambers. It took a large ego to commit oneself to such a monumental and remote monument. That Edward had succeeded was obvious from the praise Claire overheard.

"He brings the sky down to earth," a woman said in the awestruck, reverent tone Claire recognized as New Age New Mexican. "I feel like I can reach out and touch it."

"It's like black velvet," another woman answered.

"He's a genius," a man said.

"Absolutely," New Age Woman replied.

The sinuous shapes of the viewing chambers and the path winding around them reminded Claire of the work of the master Spanish architect Antoni Gaudi. Tiles were set into the path in the chevron pattern of rattlesnake hide.

Claire liked the feeling of intimacy created by the series of small chambers. The combination of path and buildings was a work of art, but the chambers themselves were geared to the sunset and the night sky and kept their secrets during daylight. One was set up to frame and light the sky, to flatten it and bring it down into the chamber, but that one worked best at sunset. Others focused on rarely occurring astral phenomena. Claire located the Venus chamber and found that it had to be entered through a low passageway as if the visitor were crawling into an igloo. She got down on her hands and knees, glad she was wearing her 501s. She poked her head into the passageway and saw a man approaching from the other side. They stared at each other like two animals on a collision course. Who had the right of way in this situation? Who had the power? Thinking the man might be uncomfortable inside and anxious to get out, Claire backed away.

"That was a trip," he said, dating himself and dusting off his pants as he crawled into daylight.

Claire crawled through the entryway and entered the chamber. The interior was painted pure white. The only light came from a small opening in the west framing the bluest patch of sky she had ever seen. The opening was on a track in the ceiling that could be moved to follow the path of Venus. She assumed it was focused on the spot where Venus would appear sometime after dark. Even in daylight, isolating a piece of sky changed the way she perceived it, turning it deeper and bluer, giving it a new meaning. Claire glanced behind her to see if there was enough light from the sky alone to cast a shadow and found there was not.

Someone hooted outside. The sound reverberated through the passageway and swirled around the chamber.

"Coming out," Claire called. She crawled

through the passageway and found a family of six waiting at the far side. "It's a small chamber," she said. "It might be better not to go in all at once."

"You first," the mother said to the father.

Claire left the viewing chambers and walked to the area in front of the spiral rocks where people were gathering as the sun moved toward the horizon. Some stood, some sat on the rocky ground, some had brought chairs or mats. Claire tried to make herself comfortable on a smooth patch of rock. Edward Girard stood in the space between the rocks as if he was a conductor preparing to orchestrate the rising of the moon. A woman with chestnut-colored hair spoke to him. She wore a trim shirt and her jeans had a crease. Edward tilted his head in her direction but his attention seemed focused on a point between the setting sun and the rising moon.

As the sky darkened, someone began drumming with a steady, repetitive beat that gave the crowd a cohesive feeling. Claire enjoyed the rare sense of being part of a tribe. There was an anticipatory rustle as the moon's aura became visible in the east. As the first sliver of light climbed over the distant mountains, the drum beat louder and the tribe cheered. The moon rose at a measured pace. Its light turned golden as more of it became visible. Edward Girard stepped aside. The moon became a perfect, golden circle that filled the space between the two rocks, an event that had been taking place every eighteen and a half years for as long as the rocks had been spirals, an event that humans had observed for thousands of years. It was a transcendent moment for Claire that reached into the past and encompassed the future. There was a collective gasp when the moon filled the space. The drum paused in its beat. From the proper angle the full moon could be seen between Spiral Rocks wherever it rose, but only the Maximum Moon filled the space.

As the moon rose higher in the sky, the tribe began to wander off. Claire stayed until it reached the very tip of the rocks. Then she stood up and shook the blood back into her numb legs. She looked around for Edward Girard but he had disappeared.

Before she went back to her truck and to sleep, she revisited the Venus Chamber. The moon was so bright now it diminished everything else in the sky. She couldn't locate Venus and doubted it would be visible inside the chamber, but she was curious to see how it looked after dark. The serpentine path was well lit by the moon and the tiles seemed to glisten and slither underfoot. Claire had the sense she was on the track of something dangerous and divine. Other people walked the path in groups or alone. If they spoke at all, their voices were hushed.

When she reached the Venus Chamber,

Claire debated whether she should hoot or howl before crawling through the passageway. Bellowing wasn't her style so she cleared her throat. When there was no answer she got down on her hands and knees and crawled in. The white interior of the chamber was dimly lit by the ambient light of the Maximum Moon, not bright enough to cast a shadow but bright enough to see that there was something in the chamber, a shaggy shape that moved and grunted like a bear. The shape lunged forward.

"Uh," it said.

"Ooh," a woman answered with a willing cry.

A couple was making love in the Venus chamber, love that was raw, powerful, dangerous, possibly even transcendent, most definitely private. Claire backed out on her hands and knees. To the people who were standing outside she said, "I'd wait before I went in there."

She returned to her truck, made herself a peanut butter sandwich, and ate it. She changed into a sweatshirt, climbed into her sleeping bag, and zipped up the zipper. But how was she supposed to sleep after that? Her dreams would be full of lusty animals transforming from men into bears. A guitar strummed in the campground. A drum beat softly. Voices laughed and sang. Claire listened until she fell asleep.

* * *

She woke up very late at night or very early in the morning when the cold white light of the moon slid into her camper shell. The campground was quiet now. Everyone else seemed to be asleep. The temperature had dropped twenty degrees. Claire was snug in her sleeping bag, but she wanted to see the monument with no one else in it. She made herself get out of bed, pulled on her hiking boots, and left the camper shell. Some people were tucked away in their tents, some were sleeping in their trucks and RVs, others were wrapped in bulky lumps of down on the ground. The moon's light made it easy to pick a path between them.

Claire looked up at the sky, where the moon was so bright that the stars had been reduced to twinkling fireflies. If the constellation Pleiades was visible, she couldn't find it.

No artificial light could be seen in the east. Spiral Rocks looked exactly as it did when the Anasazi lived nearby. Fire, the moon, the stars, and the planets were the only light they had at night. The night sky reflected the Indians' life on earth. To them the Milky Way was the tracks of the dead. The constellations were their brothers and sisters and the animals who inhabited their world. The moon was in the west now, at Claire's back, casting a long shadow before her. She followed it through the campground, toward the twin spirals.

A man stood alone between the rocks. Claire had no fear of approaching him in this enchanted time and place. When she got closer she saw that his hair was thick and shoulder length and his legs were as long as a spider's. It was the celestial artist, Edward Girard, surveying his domain.

# Chapter Fourteen

When Claire was close enough to speak, she said, "Watching the moon rise through the rocks was a magical experience. I'll remember it for the rest of my life."

Edward smiled. "Much as I'd like to do so I can take no credit for the rising of the moon."

"You can take credit for the viewing chambers. I hope they endure for centuries to come."

"Or as long as anyone is left on earth to see them," Edward said.

Claire believed the universe would continue its dance whether there were humans and animals around to notice or not. But she hadn't come to Spiral Rocks to solve that particular conundrum.

"Is the light of Venus really bright enough to cast a shadow?" she asked.

"Yes, but not when there's a full moon. Come back at the dark of the moon at a time when Venus is the Evening Star. Venus has an eight-year cycle, and the chamber is set up for viewing it at the times of maximum brilliance."

"I've heard that there are people who can

see Venus in the daytime."

"It's not that hard if you know where to look. Venus is easiest to see just before sunrise or sunset when the viewer is standing in a shadow that minimizes the effects of the sun. On the other hand the shadow of Venus may best be seen when the viewer stands in the light. That's why the inside of the chamber is painted white. Sand and snow are also good backgrounds."

It was Claire's chance to bring up the subject of Maia and she went with it. "My name is Claire Reynier. I work at the library at UNM in Albuquerque," she said. "A young woman who called herself Maia died in a basement storage room recently. Do you know anybody with that name?"

"In mythology," he said, "but not in life."

"She told me Venus could be seen in the daytime. An illustration of Spiral Rocks by the expedition artist Quentin Valor was found next to her body. It had been cut out of the library copy of *Ancient Sites*."

Edward leaned against one of the rocks and crossed his arms. "Oh?" he asked.

"Maia was a homeless person who had no identification. The police haven't been able to establish who she was or where she came from. She was medium-sized, pale, with straight brown hair and high cheekbones. She was neatly dressed."

"How old was she?"

"Around twenty, I'd say."

"Was she good-looking?"

"In a quiet way. She could have been striking if she'd made more of an effort. She acted like she didn't want to be noticed. An Albuquerque artist named Lisa Teague painted her portrait. She asked to be represented dancing in a New Mexico setting with six other girls. Considering that she called herself Maia, the painting could be seen as representing the seven daughters of Atlas and Pleione, who became the constellation Pleiades."

Edward watched and waited to see where this was going. His face had a strong bone structure. The light of the descending moon created dark shadows under his chin and deep pockets around his eyes.

From her limited supply of facts about Maia, Claire pulled out two more. "She died of a heroin overdose. She seemed to be claustrophobic."

Edward left the support of the rock and stood up straight, spacing his long legs apart for balance. "You could be describing a woman named Veronica Reid who lived here nearly twenty years ago," he said. "She had fine cheekbones and was beautiful back then. She had an interest in the stars. She was afraid of lots of things — heights, depths, shadows at sunset, the light of the moon. Mostly I'd say she was afraid of her own potential. She wanted to be an artist, but fear got in her way. Fear of failure? Fear of success? Who knows? Veronica liked drugs, but she never took heroin when I knew her."

"What happened to her?" Claire asked.

"She died in Taos a couple of years ago."

"Oh, no. How?"

"Someone sent me a clipping from the Taos paper saying she'd fallen or jumped from the Rio Grande Gorge Bridge. According to the article she didn't leave a suicide note so no one knew if her death was accidental or deliberate. Maybe she conquered her fears or maybe she gave into them. Only suicides get to choose their own death. It's how Veronica would have wanted to die, anyway. Quick and dramatic, running away from her demons."

"Who sent you the clipping?"

"I don't know. It had a Taos postmark but no return address."

"How old was Veronica when she died?" Claire asked.

"Pushing forty."

"Why did she leave Spiral Rocks?"

"The women who come here always leave," Edward said with a resigned shrug. "It's too isolated and lonely. I don't pay enough attention to them, they say. I get irritable when they interrupt me, but that never stops them from interrupting me. My first loves, they tell me, are stars and rocks. Being creative is a selfish life, but if you're truly creative you have no choice but to seek the light. Van Gogh said, I am not ashamed to say it exists, this white light — and that I seek it.' "

Claire understood how women would be attracted to the artistic Edward and also how he would drive them away. He was as magnetic and as cold as the moon.

"Veronica went to Taos and moved in with an architect there named Damon Fitzgerald. I never heard from her again," he said.

As the moon approached the horizon the shadows of the rocks lengthened until they extended over the edge of the mesa. There was a pause and a deep breath from Edward before he said, "I haven't talked about this for years and it's not an easy thing to do. Veronica and I had a daughter conceived at the last Maximum Moon, which would make her almost eighteen years old. Veronica insisted on naming her June, which I thought was a banal name. If June decided to rename herself Maia, who would blame her? When June was six months old Veronica left and that was the last time I ever saw either one of them."

That Maia could be Edward Girard's daughter was stunning news. Identifying her and connecting her to a parent made Claire feel she had dropped a burdensome backpack, but her sense of relief was tempered by

Edward's lack of connection to his daughter. "Didn't you try to find June after she left?" she asked.

"I knew they were in Taos, that they were living in the Cave Commune with the architect Damon Fitzgerald, but Veronica had started a new life and didn't want anything to do with me. She ended up hating it here. Art is a jealous wife, and when you're married to your work you don't get a divorce. If this Maia is our daughter, she resembles her mother in more than appearance — the fears, the attraction to drugs. Veronica's own mother committed suicide when she was young. When a mother kills herself it becomes a strong undertow in a child's life. In most families suicide would be unthinkable, but children of a suicide always know that option is there if they want to take it. They fear it at the same time they are drawn to it. I wasn't really surprised to learn that Veronica might have killed herself. Did Maia commit suicide, too?"

"No one knows. She didn't leave a note. Apparently she was once addicted to heroin but had kicked the habit. When she started up again, the heroin she took was very strong and rarely seen in Albuquerque. It could have been an accidental overdose."

"She was homeless, you said."

"Yes."

"Maybe she felt she had nothing left to live

for. Maybe she felt Veronica and her grandmother calling her from beyond the grave."

"She had you," Claire pointed out. "Didn't you want to look her up when you heard her mother had died?"

"What did she know about me?" Edward asked, tossing his head so his hair fell away from his shoulder. "In the clipping her name was June Reid. It's possible she didn't even know I was her father."

"It was also possible she was the one who sent you the clipping."

"Then why didn't she say so?"

"She died Memorial Day weekend with the illustration of Spiral Rocks at her side. Suppose she was planning to come here for the opening?" Claire asked him.

"Well, that would have been an experience, wouldn't it? To have a daughter I didn't know step out of the crowd. Better that than you coming here to tell me she was dead."

The moon had set behind the mountains in the west. It was early morning now, first light. Spiral Rocks was no longer under a lunar spell. A sliver of coral in the east signaled the rising sun. The birds began to sing their morning song.

"I have a copy of Lisa Teague's painting in my truck," Claire said. "Would you like to see it?"

"Over a cup of coffee?" Edward asked.

"All right."

“Meet me at the house.”

The sleeping bags had begun to stir as Claire crossed the campground. She opened her truck, picked up her folder and her book, and walked to the house.

She smelled coffee brewing as she stepped onto the porch. The house where Edward lived was ramshackle, sprawling, sparsely furnished. Claire knocked on the screen door. When no one answered, she let herself in. She found Edward in the kitchen making coffee. The light suspended over the table was fluorescent, which surprised her. She didn’t use harsh fluorescent bulbs in her own house and expected an artist to be more sensitive to light.

“I often work all night,” he said, “and drink coffee all day. I’ve got a java jones. That and my work are my addictions. Do you have any?”

“I work too hard myself,” Claire admitted.

“Sometimes it’s easier to work than it is to live,” Edward said.

“Sometimes.”

She sat down at the table and he poured her a cup of strong coffee. She opened *Ancient Sites* to show him the Quentin Valor illustration.

“I’ve seen it,” he said. “I love Valor’s work. He has a fine eye for line and detail.”

She handed him the photocopy of *Summertime* and it settled as lightly as a feather on his rough and callused hands.

"When you told me the subject of this painting I expected romantic crap, but this artist has talent." Edward's eyes were intense as they turned from the picture to Claire. "I've always wondered if my daughter was artistic."

"Is she your only child?"

"Yes," Edward said.

"When Maia lived at the Hope Central Shelter she studied with Lisa Teague. Maybe Lisa could tell you more about her."

Edward's eyes returned to the image. "Given the hollyhocks and the adobe walls, I'd say the setting of this painting is Taos."

"Did your daughter have half siblings in Taos? Is that why she asked to be painted with six other girls?" Claire was hesitant to mention the story of Coyote and the possibility of abuse to a father, even a father as remote as Edward Girard.

"June was the only child mentioned in the article I received about Veronica's death. Damon Fitzgerald sees himself as a kind of hippie Frank Lloyd Wright surrounded by adoring groupies. Veronica hated solitude. I'm sure she liked living in a commune and having lots of people around. If you ask me, Fitzgerald's one contribution to architecture has been to reinvent the cave. Veronica and I visited the commune before she got involved with him. His houses are built into the mesa with a southern exposure but they're dark and damp. Energy efficient, maybe, but miserable to live in. Not much of an accomplishment to build a career on." Edward's eyes were full of disdain.

"Your chambers remind me of caves carved out of a cliff and tipped upside down," Claire said.

"Maybe Damon and I have more in common than Veronica, but my caves are observatories, not meant to be lived in."

In dawn's sharp light Edward Girard had turned edgy. He fidgeted and seemed anxious to stop talking and get back to his work. Claire recognized that it was time to leave, but she had a few more questions.

"The painting was in the window of the Downtown Gallery in Albuquerque," she said. "A woman in her forties or fifties went into the gallery claiming she had to have it. She paid all cash. Do you have any idea who that was? Could it be someone who recognized Maia?" Claire's fantasy that the woman had been Maia's mother had come to a depressing end.

"I don't know. Veronica was an only child so it wouldn't have been anyone related to her. It might have been someone from the commune." He shrugged. "Maybe it was just someone who fell in love with the painting. That happens. There are women who fall in love with my work and mistake it for love of me. A couple of months around here disabuses anyone of that notion."

"The Albuquerque police have a photo of Maia taken after she died. Would you be willing to look at it to help them identify her?"

"How could I identify her?" Edward asked. "I haven't seen her since she was six months old."

"You could compare her appearance to Veronica's."

"True."

"Do you see any resemblance between Veronica and the girl in the painting?"

"Some," he admitted. "Will I see anything of myself in the girl in the police photo?"

Much as she would have liked to see something of Edward in Maia, Claire did not. Edward was a man who attracted attention. Maia was a woman who tried not to. Both of their faces were defined by their bone structure, but Maia's bones were fine and delicate and Edward's were coarse. Claire didn't see any similarity in the hair or the eyes, either. The one thing they had in common was that Maia's remoteness in death resembled Edward's remoteness in life. "DNA analysis could establish for sure if you're her father," was all Claire could say.

"I'll think about it," he replied.

With no warning, a woman stepped into the kitchen, startling Claire. "Sorry," the woman said to Edward, stopping in her tracks. "I didn't know you had company."

She was the woman Claire had seen talking to Edward the previous evening. It was still very early in the morning, but she was perfectly groomed. Every strand of chestnut hair was in place. Her makeup was perfect. Her jeans didn't have a wrinkle in them.

"Time to go back to the difficult part of my work," Edward said, rolling his eyes for Claire. "Jennifer Rule, meet Claire Reynier. Jennifer is my publicist. She has appointments for me to keep, right?"

"The reporter from the *Denver Post* is waiting," Jennifer said. "It's an important interview, Edward; you know that."

"I'm sure it is," he said.

"Have we met before?" Jennifer asked Claire.

Wrapped around that simple question was the more complex question of Who are you, anyway, and what are you doing alone with Edward at the crack of dawn? "We haven't actually met," Claire said. "I talked to you over the phone about coming here."

"I talk to so many people," Jennifer said, throwing her hands up in an exasperated gesture. "It's hard to remember them all. What's that?" She looked at the photocopy of the painting Edward held.

"It's a copy of a painting of a young woman who died in the basement of the library at the University of New Mexico, where Claire works," Edward said. "She brought me this."

Jennifer turned away from the picture as if it were an annoying insect that she wished would fly away without her having to learn any more about it. She seemed either remarkably uncurious or totally focused on the task of promoting Edward Girard as she changed the subject to his appointment. "The reporter's name is Laura St. James," she said to him. "She brought a photographer with her and they'd like to photograph you in a few minutes at the rocks. *If* that's all right."

"I'm afraid it is a necessary evil," Edward groaned. "Can I keep this?" he asked Claire, indicating the photocopy.

"Of course," Claire said. She handed him her card. "Could you send me a copy of the newspaper clipping?"

"If I can find it."

"Thanks for your help," she said.

"Thank you for coming."

# Chapter Fifteen

As Claire walked back across the mesa to her truck, she thought about the relationship between Edward and Jennifer. Were they merely business partners or were they also lovers? Where had Jennifer spent the night and how did she manage to be so well groomed so early in the morning? Claire's own slept-in jeans reflected every toss and turn she'd made inside her sleeping bag. Her hair, far from sleek and perfect, had fallen into the mussed-up style known in Hollywood as bed head. She had put on no makeup. Jennifer's sleek style and forceful personality seemed in opposition to Edward's laid-back reserve. But opposites attract, and one thing they had in common was ambition for Edward. Could that make Jennifer the one woman who could tolerate Edward's devotion to his work? When he succeeded, she would, too.

Other campers were packing up and leaving Spiral Rocks in the early morning light. Claire followed their dust down the winding dirt road. She was glad to finally get back on a paved highway. At the first pull-off she came to, she stopped and took out her map. Taos was out of her way but not by much. It was easier to get there from here than it would be from Albuquerque. She was tired, but now that she was on the path of learning about Maia, her adrenaline began to kick in. She'd found Maia's possible next of kin and delivered the terrible news, but instead of ending her quest it had sent it in another direction. Claire put away the map, turned her truck back onto the highway, reversed her direction, and headed southeast to Taos.

It was four hours of glorious mountain scenery and picturesque small towns, a spectacular drive from Spiral Rocks, yet Edward claimed he'd never made the trip to see his own daughter. Claire knew there were men who lived in the same town as their children and never bothered to see them. It wasn't miles that kept the dads away. It was indifference or guilt or fear — or hatred of the mothers. She also knew that different rules were likely to be applied to the very talented. If an artist created enduring and monumental work, his failings as a father or a human being would be forgiven. Claire believed that Edward's work was significant and would endure, yet his daughter might have died of an overdose, homeless and alone. What kind of legacy was that? Claire admired him as an artist but not as a parent. A parent should never have let his daughter get away; a parent should have tracked Maia down wherever she went.

Claire had heard of the Cave Commune, one of those places in New Mexico where the sixties never ended. She knew it was located somewhere between Arroyo Hondo and Taos. She took the road in from Lama and followed the signs to Cave Commune on the wide open, windswept, sagebrush mesa. Some places were too vast for human habitation and Claire considered this one. She pulled into the commune, a cluster of dwellings built into the side of a south-facing ridge. She saw a kind of desolation here, a sense of poverty and unfulfilled dreams. Dogs ran loose, yapping at each other. A string of Buddhist prayer flags flapped in the wind. The colors had faded and the edges were whipped into tatters. It surprised Claire that Damon Fitzgerald was considered the architect and Edward Girard the artist. Girard's domes had pleasing proportions and were carefully placed. Fitzgerald's houses were not well situated and they seemed unfinished. They looked like dwellings where the skylights leaked and let in cold air, houses that were always cold and damp — not an easy feat to accomplish in New Mexico. Claire saw imagination here, but she also saw carelessness. She parked her truck and climbed out to greet the barking dogs.

A young woman came out of one of the cave houses balancing a baby on her hip. She looked like she belonged more on Central

Avenue than in the high clear air of Taos. Her style was similar to Lisa Teague's but even more streetwise. The thighs of her jeans were sandblasted white. Her red tank top had spaghetti straps that didn't even try to cover the straps of her black bra. Her hair was held loosely in place with a plastic butterfly clip. She had golden rings in the side of her nose and a stud marking the middle of her tongue. It wasn't a look Claire expected to find in Taos. She'd been expecting tired hippie gear, but she reminded herself that every generation has to defy its parents' rules and reinvent the blue jean.

"Shut up," the girl said to the dogs. "Hey," she said to Claire.

"Hello," Claire replied.

"Can I help you?"

"I'm looking for information about a girl named June Reid who used to live here."

"Sure, I knew June. We were good friends, but she left after her mother died and she never came back."

"Her mother was Veronica?"

"Yeah." The girl shooed the dogs away and began to bounce the baby up and down in her arms. It amused the infant, who smiled and giggled, but the bouncing made Claire nervous.

"How did she die?" Claire asked, checking Edward's story.

"She jumped into the Rio Grande Gorge.

It was a shitty thing to do, if you ask me. She coulda hung on for her daughter's sake."

"Veronica killed herself?"

"That's what I think. The police say she coulda fallen, but who falls accidentally into the Rio Grande Gorge unless they've already got one foot over the edge? Things got tough and Veronica gave up." She started swinging the baby back and forth headfirst, as if it was about to become a guided missile. Claire cringed.

"What kind of things?" she asked.

"Oh . . . things," the girl said.

"I have a copy of a painting by an artist in Albuquerque. Could you tell me whether it's a picture of June?"

"Sure."

The girl's arms were busy with the baby, so Claire pulled the picture out of the folder and held it in front of her eyes.

"Yup, that's June all right," the girl said, "when she was around twelve or thirteen. She was so pretty then, just like her mother. She coulda been a model, but she stopped taking care of herself after her mother died. That girl there with the black hair all the way down her back is Sophie Roybal. That girl on the right is me. So many of the girls have left now. There's no one left to hang with anymore."

"Maureen!" A woman yelled from the doorway of the house. "Who's that you're talking to?"

The woman came out of the house and the dogs began barking again. She had the worn sixties look Claire had expected to find — faded jeans, sandals, and a T-shirt without a bra. Her breasts wriggled like a litter of puppies as she walked. She was Maureen forty pounds heavier, thirty years older. Maureen with a hostile attitude.

"This lady's lookin' for June Reid," Maureen said.

By now the woman stood next to them. "Stop bouncing the baby," she told Maureen.

"Sure, Ma," the girl responded, catching the baby and hugging it in her arms.

"Why are you looking for June?" the mother asked, adding more creases to her already weathered face as she narrowed her eyes and squinted at Claire.

"I'm not looking *for* her. I'm looking for information about her. I work at the library at UNM in Albuquerque. A homeless woman died recently in a storage room in the basement. She left no ID, but I have reason to believe it was June."

"Aw, shit!" Maureen cried, squeezing the baby tight. "June died?" Echoing her distress, the baby began to whimper.

Claire showed the older woman the picture. "An artist in Albuquerque painted this picture of the woman who died. Can you tell me if it's June?" The reaction she'd been getting from the picture was turning into her own jolt of java that kept her alert on a day when exhaustion might have turned her into a stone.

"Who knows? It could be anybody," the woman said, burying her reaction in another squint.

"C'mon, Ma," Maureen said. "You know that's June." She pointed at the picture. "That's Sophie Roybal and that's me."

"I don't know that," the woman said. "You can't even see the other girls' faces. If June died, it would be sad, but I can't say that's a picture of her or anybody else I know. Come on, Maureen, let's take the baby inside. She's getting too much sun."

"Is Damon Fitzgerald around?" Claire asked.

"He doesn't live here anymore," the woman said, turning away from Claire.

"He lives in town now on —", Maureen began.

"I said go inside," her mother interrupted.

"It's no big deal, Ma. Everybody knows where Damon lives."

"Go inside," her mother insisted. She put her hand on Maureen's back, guiding her and the baby into the house, where she shut the door behind them.

If there was a deadbolt, Claire had no doubt it had clicked into place. The mother's actions had raised a number of questions but had ended any further investigation at Cave Commune.

# Chapter Sixteen

Claire got back into her truck and drove into town. Taos was still small enough that a few queries were all it took to locate Damon Fitzgerald. At the third convenience store she found someone to give her directions to where he lived. The combination of bad road and magnificent houses reminded her of the saying in Santa Fe that the better the neighborhood, the worse the road. Damon had gone from a cave house worth maybe a hundred thousand dollars to a mud hut worth at least half a million. His new residence was a beautifully restored, sprawling adobe with a hand-carved door that was a work of art in itself.

Claire parked and walked up to the door, wondering whether he'd found out about her visit to the compound yet. It wouldn't take any time to make a phone call from there to here.

A woman with a round, smooth face came to the door. It was a face that had no visible bone structure, one that appeared to reflect back what others thought before it expressed the woman's own desires. Her pale hair was pulled back in a knot. She wore a pink cotton sundress. Her friendly manner suggested that she didn't consider Claire a threat.

"Hello," the woman said.

"Hello," Claire responded. "I'm looking for Damon Fitzgerald. Is he here?"

"He's working in his studio. Can I help?"

"I'd like to talk to him."

"What's it about?"

"June Reid."

Anxiety ruffled the placid surface of the woman's face. "I'll get him. What did you say your name was?"

"Claire Reynier. I work at UNM library in Albuquerque. And you are?"

"Sharon Miller. Just a minute," the woman said, but it took several minutes for her to return. Claire waited at the door. She watched a truck approach and stir up a cloud of dust. She listened to a dog bark and a raven caw. She admired the distant purple mountains.

Eventually the door reopened and the woman said, "Come in."

She led Claire down a hallway with a polished wooden floor, through a living room decorated with elegant antiques, into a room at the back of the house furnished in a kind of fifties kitsch with plastic bucket chairs that were amusing to look at but uncomfortable to sit in. The door on the far side of the room opened onto a lush rose garden. The door was open and a man stood in front of it wearing a faded T-shirt and paint-splattered pants. His hair was thick and curly — black with gray highlights. His eyes were a startling sapphire blue. He wasn't tall — about five feet ten — but he had broad shoulders and muscular arms. His stomach, however, showed the beginnings of a paunch. He had a forceful and dynamic presence that seemed too large for this room, too large for this house, maybe even too large for Taos.

"I'm Damon Fitzgerald," he said, stepping into the room and extending a paint-stained hand.

"Claire Reynier," she replied.

"What is it you do at UNM?"

"I'm a librarian and an archivist at the Center for Southwest Research."

"That's at Zimmerman, right?"

"Right."

"People always think of Zimmerman as a temple to higher learning. It was a major commission for John Gaw Meem. He could have broken away from those boring Southwest conventions — the vigas, the corbels, the endless latillas — and done something bold and original. Even in his day the Southwest style was ripe for reinvention."

Comparing all Meem had accomplished to what she'd seen of Fitzgerald's work, Claire considered those words to be blarney, but Damon spoke them in a resonant baritone voice that could sway the unbeliever, lull children to sleep, and lure women into bed. Sharon's head was tilted slightly as she listened with a rapt and adoring expression. If Damon was on the lecture circuit, that might have paid for this house. Or was it Sharon's house? Claire figured they were her antiques.

"Did you go to UNM?" Claire asked Damon.

"No. I went to Stanford, but I've lectured at UNM. Sharon told me you asked about June Reid?"

"Yes."

"I haven't seen her in ages. She left town after her mother died. What is it you want to know about June?" He blinked his blue eyes disingenuously, calling attention to his thick black eyelashes. Claire had the sensation that there was a mirror on the wall behind her where Damon monitored his own performance. The feeling was so strong she was tempted to turn around and check, but she kept her eyes on Damon while she told her story.

"A homeless woman was found dead in a storage room under the library. I have been trying to identify her and I now believe it's June." It was one more shot of adrenaline for Claire. As long as she went on talking about June Reid's death, she could stay awake forever. She hoped that being energized by death wouldn't become habitual.

"No!" Damon said, shaking his mane of tousled hair. "That's terrible. What happened to her?"

Claire gave him credit for the performance, but she didn't believe this was the first he'd heard of June's death. There was plenty of time for Maureen's mother or someone else to have called him from the commune, plenty of time to have prepared this act. She looked to Sharon and found that her reaction mirrored Damon's, although not as professionally.

"She died of a heroin overdose," Claire said.

"Did you know her well?" Damon asked.

"I met her a few times."

"How did she end up homeless in Albuquerque? I helped to raise that girl. Where was her father, Edward Girard?"

"He told me he lost touch with her after Veronica moved to Taos."

"That's bullshit. Veronica stayed in touch with him. She sent him pictures of June, but Edward couldn't be bothered to come down off his mountaintop to see his own daughter. He's a coldhearted son of a bitch. His monument leaves no room for people in his life."

"You know him?"

"We've met. June told me she contacted Edward after Veronica died. Edward should have been there for her at that time. She could have moved to Spiral Rocks if she was broke. She didn't have to end up homeless in Albuquerque."

Veronica had had two artistic men in her life and now they'd given Claire two different versions of events. One of them was lying at worst, concealing facts at best. Damon had more flair, but did that make him a better liar? "What happened to Veronica?" Claire asked. "How did she die?"

"She fell off her horse and injured her back. She was in a lot of pain and started using, then abusing, Percocet. She couldn't break the habit. She got depressed and she threw herself into the Taos Gorge. It was a rotten thing to do to June, who hung around the commune for a while but eventually left. Sounds like she ended up in Albuquerque abusing drugs, just like her mother."

"She called herself Maia while she was in Albuquerque."

"Why?"

"Maia was a figure in Greek mythology who escaped into the sky to get away from the attentions of Orion the hunter."

"June was a looker, just like her mother. I'm sure she was pursued by men wherever she went unless she got heavily into drugs. Drugs will ruin a woman's looks for sure." Damon worked his thick lashes. "You kind of remind me of them, the same pale coloring, the same high cheekbones."

He smiled at Claire, but she resisted his

charm, glancing over at Sharon to see how she was taking the flattery and the conversation's focus on Veronica and June. Not well, was Claire's impression. Sharon was the moon to Damon Fitzgerald's sun, but her expression reflected an uneasiness not visible in Damon's practiced smile. Claire was reminded that the moon had peaks and valleys and shadows of its own.

A bird popped out of a kitschy cuckoo clock on the wall to announce the hour. The timing was so perfect that Claire imagined it had been set off by a remote.

"Anything else?" Damon asked. "I'm pretty busy right now."

"That's all," Claire said.

"Good to meet you. Stay in touch," Damon said, squeezing her hand.

His attention had been focused on Claire throughout the conversation. She hadn't seen him glance at Sharon once, although Sharon had not taken her eyes off him. He turned toward her now. "Would you take Claire to the door?" he asked.

"Of course," Sharon said. She walked Claire back through the house and let her out the front door.

Claire was glad to be out of the house and into her truck. She was looking forward to going home, but she had one more stop to make before leaving Taos. Instead of turning south in the direction of Albuquerque, she turned north and drove through the village toward the place where the river had sliced a deep gash through the sagebrush mesa and the bridge straddled the gorge to the place where Veronica Reid had died.

# Chapter Seventeen

There were parking lots on three corners of the bridge and a picnic area with restrooms on the fourth. Claire pulled into the empty lot on her side of the road. Barbed wire marked the edge of the lot and the beginning of Taos Pueblo land. She parked her truck, got out, and walked up to the bridge, which had sidewalks on both sides. The railing was chest height with protrusions in the middle of the bridge where pedestrians could look down several hundred feet into the depths of the gorge. A woman stood on the far side taking pictures. Her blond hair, a magnet for sunlight, made golden promises in the landscape of muted green sage and black volcanic rock. Claire imagined June's mother, Veronica, standing on this bridge with her hair blowing in the wind. She'd been a beauty, a "looker," a word used by men who thought a woman's purpose was to look good on their arms. Damon had said that Claire resembled Veronica. Was that why Maia told her she looked beautiful, or was that just BS on Damon's part? He was a man who'd be capable of flattery if he thought he could benefit from it — at least until someone else caught his eye. Edward hadn't told Claire she resembled Veronica, but then he'd said he hadn't seen her in almost twenty years.

Claire had come here thinking that if she could understand Veronica's death, she could understand why Maia — June — died the way she did. On the surface both seemed like suicides, but this was a place where the surface had a deep crack in it. If there was another way to look at Veronica's death, it might be found by walking a mile in her shoes. Claire stepped onto the bridge and a passing car caused a tremor beneath her feet. She gripped the railing but that trembled, too. The blond woman had returned to her car and driven away. There was no one else on the bridge. In the east clouds were building up over Wheeler Peak. Lightning flashed and Claire felt electricity zing through the railing. She released her grip and walked to the middle of the bridge with her hands at her sides and her eyes on the pavement.

When she reached the lookout, she raised her eyes to the wild and vast landscape. When she was younger the wide openness of this place would have caused rats to gnaw at her stomach. Her heart would have been racing, her palms sweating. She would have been pierced by the fear that she would harm herself or someone else if she didn't flee, but once a woman started to run, she might never stop. Running turned a woman into prey. Claire gripped the rail and made herself look into the depths of the gorge, down, down, down into the place where the rocks met a ribbon of bronze river. She'd heard rafters' accounts that the riverbanks were littered with the wrecks of canoes and of vehicles that had rolled off the edge of the mesa. It was a place that tempted the reckless and the unhinged. Many people had died here. Their spirits seemed to linger in the gorge and whisper on the wind.

Claire wondered if Veronica had come here intending to kill herself or if the gorge had exerted an irresistible pull that sucked her in. The railing was an obstacle that could be climbed over, but nobody accidentally fell from this bridge. Death in this place was a deliberate act. Why did a woman who was afraid of heights choose this spot to die? Why not shut herself up in a room with her drugs the way her daughter had? Claire could imagine the terror an acrophobic person would feel staring into the gorge. Maybe Veronica wanted to rid herself of all her fears and her *ansia* had pulled her in.

Claire's thoughts were interrupted by a cackling sound. At first she thought it was a raven, but then a couple stepped onto the southern edge of the bridge, shoving each other and laughing. Claire hadn't solved anything. She didn't want her thoughts to be interrupted by laughter. She yielded her place to the couple and walked off the bridge.

There were three vehicles in the parking area now — her truck, an SUV, another truck. Since she needed to use the restroom before heading home, she got into her truck and drove across the bridge. After she used the facilities, she decided to take a walk along a trail that followed the rim to stretch her legs before the long drive back to Albuquerque. Walking on the trail felt far more natural than walking on the bridge. There was nothing to hold on to, but the ground didn't shimmy beneath her every time a vehicle passed by. She saw a few places where the mesa ended abruptly at the gorge, but mostly a series of sage-dotted ledges led down to the river. The color of the water changed from green to bronze to brown as her perspective shifted. Sometimes the water had no color of its own but was a shimmering reflection of the sky.

Claire enjoyed the walk and went farther than she had intended. When she noticed that her shadow was lengthening beside her, she knew it was time to head for home. She turned toward her car and saw a man, wearing jeans and a blue T-shirt, approaching on the footpath. He was slender and medium-sized with short and straight brown hair. He had a quick, alert way of walking, like a boxer balancing lightly on the balls of his feet.

"Hey," he called out.

Claire had been so deep in her thoughts that she had the sensation the man was a vision or a dream. She blinked but he didn't go away. She didn't relish meeting a man in such an isolated place. No one else was in sight on the rim. The path was too narrow to circle around him. It would be foolish to run. There was nothing to do but stand still and watch him approach.

The man stopped and extended his hand palm up in the conciliatory gesture used to calm an anxious dog. "I didn't mean to alarm you," he said. "I'm sorry. I just want to talk for a few minutes."

He was close enough now for Claire to see the tension that wasn't evident in his movements chiseled into his face. His forehead rippled with worry. "What about?" she asked.

"June Reid. I heard you were asking about her."

"June's dead," Claire replied. She was too tired to put a bouquet of pretty words on this piece of bad news.

"So I heard."

"How did you know I was asking about her?"

"A woman at the commune called and told me you'd been there."

"What woman?" Claire asked, thinking it must have been Maureen.

"She asked me not to say. She told me you

might be going to Damon Fitzgerald's house. I saw your truck parked out front. I waited and I followed you here. It took me a while to get up my courage to talk to you. I thought you'd be alarmed if I approached you on the bridge, and then that couple showed up. I'm sorry if I frightened you." He pointed into the gorge at a point well south of the bridge. "That's where June's mother Veronica died."

"I thought she jumped off the bridge."

"Who told you that?"

"June's father, Edward Girard. He said he read it in a newspaper clipping someone sent him."

"It's not true. I was on the search-and-rescue crew that pulled her body out of the gorge. A rafter saw it there and called us."

"Could the river have washed the body downstream?"

"No. Veronica landed on the riverbank, not in the water. She never even got wet. If she jumped, she jumped from Buffalo Point." He pointed to a place where the mesa jutted into the gorge.

"She killed herself?" Claire asked.

The man left pauses of doubt between his words. "No note was found. The police ruled it an accidental death. Veronica had reason to commit suicide, so everyone assumes that's what happened."

"Oh?" Claire asked.

The man's hands were at his sides and he clenched his fists. His shadow lengthened beside him, reaching toward the gorge. "Her former lover Damon Fitzgerald had sex with her daughter, June."

Claire felt the ground was falling away and leaving her standing perilously close to the edge. It was deeply shocking news, yet in a way it made perfect sense, like finding the one uniquely shaped piece that fit the hole in the heart of the puzzle. As Claire had suspected Maia/June was "a girl who." "How old was June when that happened?" she asked.

"Twelve."

The age in the painting, the dangerous age.

"Damon thought he was a Peter Pan who would never grow old. He had a good idea once and a chance to make it big, but he lost a couple of major commissions. To feed his ego he turned to seducing young women. Ecstasy helped."

"He slept with his lover's daughter?" Claire asked. It would be step-incest, one stage removed from the ultimate taboo — real incest. Damon Fitzgerald was the shadow in the corner of the painting, the relative who turned into a bear.

"His former lover. He and Veronica had broken up by then. June said it happened several times, but Damon would only admit to once to Veronica and to nothing to the DA."

Claire had heard the "once" excuse before. Whatever men did wrong, they only admitted to doing it once. Why did they think once was any different from ten thousand times? "Was that why he moved into town?"

"Yeah. Damon said the sex was consensual and June didn't deny it, but the scandal tore the Cave Commune apart. Damon moved into town and eventually found Sharon Miller to support him. She was new to Taos and didn't know any better. Damon talks a good game. He's magnetic, and in the free-love atmosphere of the commune he was king. Some women find him irresistible, but he's scum and love is never free. Damon didn't think there was anything wrong with having sex with underage girls, even a girl who was the daughter of his lover." The man put his hand over his eyes to shield them from the sinking sun. "Could I see the picture you have of June and the girls dancing?"

"I'd like to know who you are first and why you want to see it," Claire said.

"My name is Bill Hartley. I teach skiing in the winter, work construction in the summer. Damon had sex with my daughter." He clenched his fists again, tightening the muscles in his forearms.

"All right." Claire was glad to move away from Buffalo Point, but she wasn't willing to walk next to Bill on the edge of the precipice. She wasn't comfortable with him walking behind her, either. "You go first," she said.

He walked quickly with an athlete's fluid grace, never once turning back to see if Claire followed. When they reached her truck she unlocked the cab, took the picture out of the folder, and handed it to him.

Although there was little wind, the picture fluttered in his hands. "That's my daughter, Rose," he said, pointing to one of the girls. Her face wasn't visible, but she had her father's medium-brown hair. "I want to know how my daughter ended up in this picture."

"June asked an artist in Albuquerque to paint her with six other girls dancing in a circle. She described the other girls and herself as she was when she was twelve." Claire stared at the girls in their white dresses. "Did Damon sleep with all of these girls?"

"I don't know. I only know he slept with my daughter, Sophie Roybal, and June. Sophie wouldn't talk to me about it. She's moved to Durango."

"Did all those girls live in the commune?"

"No. After the scandal Damon moved into town and had sex with some of the town girls, including my daughter. I complained to the district attorney, Allana Bruno, but she said it would be very difficult to get a conviction in Rose's case because she was sixteen at the time. She's twenty now. Allana needed a victim younger than thirteen to convict

Damon of criminal sexual penetration in the first degree. The only way she could get a conviction for Rose was if she would testify that she was raped. But Rose wasn't willing to do that. That scumbag took away my daughter's innocence, and I want him to pay for it. The DA brought him in and got him to agree to counseling, but that's nothing. He meets once a week with other sex offenders, only he doesn't think he's like them. In my opinion he's just like every pedophile priest who took advantage of his power." The photocopy of the picture rattled in his hands like a dead leaf.

"What became of your daughter?" Claire asked.

"She's working in Denver and getting her life together. But my wife and I are still here. This is our home. Why should we have to leave? Taos is a small town and everywhere I go I see Damon Fitzgerald. I can't even pump gas without running into the son of a bitch. June was my only hope for putting him in jail. Because she was twelve the criminal sexual penetration was a first-degree felony, which could mean life in prison. There's no statute of limitations on first-degree felonies. It took me a long time to track June down but a friend of Rose's saw her on the street in Albuquerque carrying her belongings around in plastic bags. I went down there to find her and talk to her."

"When?" Claire asked.

"In May. I went to the homeless shelters but no one would tell me anything. They think a man who is looking for a woman on the street wants to cause trouble. I started asking street people and I met one who knew June and knew where she hung out. I found her in the public library on Copper."

"Was she on drugs?"

"She seemed straight to me. June was a smart girl. She told me she spent her days in the libraries reading and studying. She hated Damon. She said she and Veronica had a horrible fight over him and she blamed herself for her mother's death. I don't think she ever recovered from that."

Does anyone ever recover from the suicide of a mother? Claire asked herself. Especially in those circumstances?

"She said she never wanted to come back to Taos or to see Damon ever again. I pleaded with her." Bill crunched the picture in his hand until the paper crumpled into peaks and valleys. "I told her she owed Rose and the other girls, but she was stubborn. I got angry. I yelled at June, and I shouldn't have done that. The librarian came and asked me to leave the library. That was the last I saw of June."

He shifted his weight from one foot to the other and stared at the paper as if surprised to see it had become a model of a mountain range. "I'm sorry," he said. "I hope you have another copy."

"Don't worry about it," Claire said. "You were asking a fragile young person to do something very difficult."

"I know. Maybe I shouldn't have pushed so hard. But later she called me and said she had set up an appointment with Allana Bruno, only she didn't show up. I never heard anything more until you turned up looking for information about her. Why? Was she a friend of yours?"

"I only met her twice." Claire explained the events that had brought her to Taos. "Did June mention her father when you talked to her?"

"No. I didn't know who her father was. I'm sure he would be angry as hell to know that Damon Fitzgerald had sex with his twelve-year-old daughter."

How angry would Edward be? thought Claire. As angry as Bill Hartley? Was Edward emotionally connected enough to his daughter to feel anger or anything else?

"Who was the person who told you where to find June?" she asked.

"A woman on the street with dyed red hair. I don't know her name."

"Where did you find her?"

"She was sleeping in the backseat of a parked car near Central. She knew June well enough to know where she hung out. How exactly did June die?"

"Of a heroin overdose. She went into a storage room to sleep or to shoot up."

"Did she leave a note?" Bill asked. His eyes, which had remained focused on Claire so far, began to circle around the mesa.

Claire saw guilt in the eye movement as if Bill feared his confrontation with June might have driven her over the edge. "There was no note," she replied. "June — who was known as Maia on the street — injected a strong type of heroin not usually seen in Albuquerque. Apparently she hadn't used for a while. Maybe she'd become more sensitive to the effects of the drug." She didn't say that something — or somebody — had driven June to start using again. Deepening lines in Bill's forehead indicated he might already have considered that. On the other hand, facial lines always deepened in New Mexico as the sun neared the horizon.

The day was ending and Claire's adrenaline was running out. She'd delivered and heard enough bad news for one day. "I need to get back to Albuquerque," she said, handing him her card. "Could I have your number? The APD is investigating and they may want to get in touch with you."

"Sure." She handed him a pen and he wrote down his number on the back of one of her cards. He handed her the scrunched-up picture. "Sorry about that."

"It's all right. I have other copies. Would you like me to send you one?"

"No. I don't want to be reminded."

They said good-bye. Claire got in her truck and drove back across the Rio Grande Gorge Bridge.

# Chapter Eighteen

She passed through the village of Taos, down the fast food strip that could have been anywhere USA, and across the mesa. The road snaked down to the level of the river. The sun hadn't quite set yet, but the canyon was already in deep shadow. There were narrow places where she passed through roadside villages. Even narrower places where there was nothing but the river on one side of her and a slippery slope on the other. Boulders broke free from their moorings here and rolled down the talus slope, picking up rocks as they fell and occasionally crashing into vehicles. Claire remembered Bill's hands crushing the picture of the dancing girls. He didn't want to be reminded by this picture, yet he remained in Taos where he would always be reminded, as long as Damon was in town. Bill Hartley was smaller than Damon but he appeared quicker and more athletic. Bill was not getting a paunch. He seemed capable of winning a physical contest if it came to that, but he hadn't taken that path. He'd internalized his anger and it was consuming him.

Claire thought his anger might be considered excessive, but she didn't know his daughter. A sixteen-year-old girl could be very experienced these days or she might not. Apparently the law didn't do much to protect sixteen-year-olds from consensual encounters, but it did protect girls who were twelve. Another father who had cause for lawful anger was Edward Girard. Claire would have to tell him what she had learned in Taos. She wished she could do it in person to see his reaction. Why had he told her he'd read that Veronica jumped off the bridge? Was that detail a lie, was it artistic license, or had he gotten the facts confused over the years? Claire knew now that Damon Fitzgerald had lied about June and was likely to do it again if he thought he could get away with it. It was also possible that Bill Hartley had been lying. It would be easy enough to find the newspaper article and get the facts about where Veronica had died. Easy, too, to call the Taos County DA and get the facts about June and Damon Fitzgerald.

Claire thought about men, lies, and anger as she drove through the narrow part of the canyon. The fact that she and June were both twelve when they were abused was one more link. Her thoughts took a switchback turn to her own unanswerable questions. What would her father have done if she'd told him about George Hogan? He would have been hurt and angry, but she doubted he would have physically attacked George; he was too civilized. If there was a bear inside her father, Claire had never seen it. The anger would have churned around inside him the way it was inside Bill Hartley. Her family had some legal recourse, which might have brought some resolution. Bill Hartley did not. He had to rely on others to file a complaint, and now there was one less girl to come forward.

It was tragic if his anger had been the straw that broke Maia/June's fragile back. If Bill Hartley's story was true, she'd had sex with her mother's lover and sometime after the news came out her mother was found dead in the Rio Grande Gorge. What kind of a burden was that for a girl to carry around? If heroin was available, it would have been all too easy to take it to ease the pain.

Claire's instinct was to believe Bill Hartley's story. His pain seemed too raw and real to be manufactured. There was one benefit that might have come from Damon's remaining in Taos. In a sense the tension between him and Bill had produced a stalemate. It was doubtful Damon would try to have sex with another young girl in Taos with the DA and Bill Hartley watching. But there was nothing to stop him from leaving Taos and doing it again. Sexual offenders were repeat offenders.

Darkness entered the gorge and Claire turned on her headlights. There had been no trial for George Hogan, no confrontation, no expressed anger, no punishment, which gave Claire her own backpack loaded with guilt to lug around. Her actions had protected her and her father but had left George Hogan free to molest again. Like the boulders that tumbled over the top of the gorge, picking up momentum as they fell, sexual abuse had repercussions until everybody in its path was flattened or dead. Claire, who would always regret she'd done nothing to stop George, thought of ways to prevent Damon from abusing again.

By the time she got home she was completely out of adrenaline. Ignoring the pleas of her cat, she fell into bed, slept through the night, and didn't wake up till eight thirty in the morning. Claire was going to be late for work, but that wasn't the first thing on her mind. She made a cup of coffee, sat down at her dining room table, and called Allana Bruno in Taos. First she spoke to the DA's assistant, explained who she was, and said that she had information about June Reid. Claire waited until the DA herself came to the phone before she would reveal what the information was.

Allana Bruno's manner was crisp and businesslike until Claire said that she believed the woman found dead in the library storage room was June Reid.

"Well, that's terrible news," Allana said, revealing a soft center beneath her crusty surface. "Terrible for June, terrible for me, terrible for everyone else. Can you tell me how and when she died?"

"It happened on Memorial Day weekend. The APD believes she died of a drug overdose." Claire told Allana how to get in touch with Detective Owen.

"Are you positive the woman who died is June?"

"I met Edward Girard, who believes he is June's father, in Colorado. He told me June had lived in the Cave Commune. I showed a painting of the woman who died to a woman named Maureen there. Later I met Bill Hartley. She and Bill both identified the woman in the painting as June Reid."

"Was the woman you talked to Maureen Prescott?"

"I didn't get her last name."

"Young, streetwise woman with a baby?"

"That's her."

"Did you tell Bill that June was dead?"

"Yes."

"What was his reaction?"

"He was tense and angry. He said he had spoken to her about contacting you. He told me that Damon Fitzgerald had sex with June, with Bill's daughter, and with other young girls in Taos and at the commune. That June's mother apparently killed herself by jumping into the Rio Grande Gorge from Buffalo Point. Is that true?"

"Veronica Reid's body was found on the riverbank below Buffalo Point," was all that Allana was willing to admit. "I have information that Damon Fitzgerald had sex with underage girls, but I can't prosecute unless one of the younger ones is willing to come forward and testify. In northern New Mexico having sex with a willing sixteen-year-old is not a prosecutable crime. I was hoping June would testify. Since she was only twelve when the act took place, that makes it a first-degree felony and there is no statute of limitations for first-degree felonies. June made an appointment to see me. She didn't show up. Now I know why."

"Is Sophie Roybal a possibility?"

Allana's voice turned guarded again. "How do you know about Sophie?"

"She's in the painting and was identified, too."

"I'd like to have a copy of that painting."

"I'll fax you one."

"Things could change, but at the moment I would have to say that Sophie Roybal is not a possibility. I'll get in touch with Detective Owen."

Claire had the sense that the clock was ticking for Allana Bruno. Time would not be money as it was for a lawyer in private practice but it was still valuable.

"Thank you for calling," Allana said. "I appreciate your help."

Claire finished her coffee, picked up the phone, took it into the living room, and sat down on the sofa. Now that Damon's abuse of Edward Girard's daughter had been confirmed, she had to tell Edward. This was a far more difficult call to make. She stared out the window and watched cloud shadows climb the Sandia Mountains before she dialed the number.

"Spiral Rocks," a woman answered. "This is Jennifer Rule."

Claire gave her name and said, "I met you on Sunday." Was it possible that was only yesterday? she asked herself. So much had happened since yesterday morning.

"I met a lot of people over the weekend," Jennifer replied. "Could you refresh my memory?"

"I was talking to Edward in the kitchen in the morning."

"Oh. You're the woman from Albuquerque who brought the painting of the girls. Right?"

"Right."

"Edward's working. He hates to be interrupted. Is there something I could help you with?" Jennifer was acting like the guardian at Edward's gate whose role was to keep the intruders away when he wanted to work.

"It's about his daughter," Claire said. "Tell Edward I have information about his daughter."

"I can pass it on," Jennifer said.

Claire was determined to get her information to Edward himself. "I need to talk to him," she insisted.

Jennifer gave in, sighed, and said, "One moment."

Many shadows climbed the mountain before Edward picked up the phone and said "Yes?" with a this-better-be-worth-the-interruption tone.

Claire told him all she had learned on her visit to Taos.

"You're telling me that Damon Fitzgerald screwed my lover, then my daughter?" was his response.

"Apparently." Was it the ultimate insult from one man to another to sleep with his mate or to abuse his daughter? Claire wondered. In this case Damon had done both. On the other hand Edward had done little to protect them.

"That bastard is still living in Taos?" he asked.

"He left the commune and is living in town with a woman named Sharon Miller."

Edward's laugh was a short, rough bark. "I suppose he thinks he resembles Frank Lloyd Wright in more ways than one. Wright also thought he could screw anybody he wanted to. How old was my daughter when this happened?"

"Twelve."

"Twelve years old. Christ! She was just a child."

"She was young enough for it to be a first-degree felony. Apparently there were other young girls, too. I found some who were also represented in the painting. Allana Bruno, the DA in Taos, wants to prosecute, but she needs a young victim to get a conviction."

"Can you imagine the attention prosecuting Damon would get? It probably wouldn't hurt him — scandal never hurt Frank Lloyd Wright, either — but it would be a nightmare for the girls and for their parents. I suppose that's why Veronica jumped off the bridge."

"Are you sure she jumped off the . . . bridge?"

"That's what it said in the article I got. If someone was trying to warn me about Damon when they sent me that, the warning was too subtle. I didn't get it."

"The information I got was that Veronica wasn't near the bridge, that her body was found south of there below Buffalo Point."

"Well, it wouldn't be the first time a newspaper got something wrong, would it? There's going to be an article in the *Denver Post* next weekend about the Maximum Moon celebration. They'll probably get something wrong, too."

Claire had decided it would be easier to find the Taos article herself than to wait for it to come from Edward. She continued her account. "Prodded by Bill Hartley, the father of another girl involved with Damon, June made an appointment to talk to Allana Bruno, but she died before she could keep it."

"No one likes to think his child could end up a heroin addict, even when the mother could never stay away from drugs, but I can understand why June might prefer heroin to standing up in court and saying she had sex with her mother's lover. How could her mother have been so stupid as to let that happen?"

The corollary to that question was how could her father have been so distant as not to know it was happening? But Claire kept that thought to herself.

"Tell your police detective that I'll do the DNA test," Edward said. "If it proves June is my daughter, I'd like to bring her back here and give her a proper burial, at least."

"I'll pass that on," Claire said. "Damon Fitzgerald told me Veronica stayed in touch with you and sent you pictures of June."

"Damon Fitzgerald is a liar. You can't believe anything he says."

"He also said June told him she contacted you after Veronica died."

"Maybe she's the one who sent me the article. If so, she didn't identify herself. Anything else? I need to get back to work."

The rocks and the sky were waiting, Claire thought. "That's all," she said.

# Chapter Nineteen

When she got to the center, Claire called Detective Owen but she wasn't in. She left a message, then walked down the hall to see Celia, who was wearing an embroidered Guatemalan huipil today. It would have made Claire feel like a macaw, but it looked great on Celia.

"Let's get a cup of coffee," Claire said.

Celia took this, as Claire knew she would, as a signal there was something that needed to be discussed outside the office. "All right," she said. "Where?"

"Book Ends."

They walked out to the cart near the main entrance, bought some coffee, and sat down at one of the tiny wrought iron tables.

"How was Spiral Rocks?" Celia asked, stirring sugar into her coffee.

"Amazing," Claire said. "The Maximum Moon came up right between the rocks just like it was supposed to. Edward Girard acted like he was conducting a performance."

Celia laughed. "The full moon rising between two penis rocks. Imagine the significance of that! What was Edward like?"

"Remote. Devoted to his work, which is

magnificent. He's building an observatory that will last through the ages. He believes that Maia is his daughter."

Celia stopped stirring her coffee and put down her spoon. "Oh, my God. Edward Girard's daughter. Well, that explains why she had the illustration."

"Edward says he hasn't seen her since she was an infant. The mother, Veronica Reid, took her to Taos to live in the Cave Commune. She and Damon Fitzgerald were lovers. Maia's real name is June Reid."

"The mother likes artistic types, doesn't she?"

"Do you know Damon Fitzgerald?"

"Only by reputation, which is that he is very impressed with himself."

Claire put her coffee cup down on the table. "Did you know that he molested underage girls? One of them was Maia."

"That pig. He slept with both the mother and the daughter? No wonder Maia OD'd on heroin. That's a hell of a thing to do to your mother."

"Veronica may have killed herself, too." Claire told Celia about her encounter with Bill Hartley at the Rio Grande Gorge Bridge.

"Whoever would have thought that all that stuff was going on in Taos? It's such a beautiful place."

"It has been kept under wraps until a young enough girl could be found to testify.

If it ever came to trial there would be plenty of publicity, which makes it even more difficult for the victims to come forward. Bill Hartley told me he met with Maia in Albuquerque and she agreed to tell the DA her story, but then she died in the storage room. He's very angry."

"You can't blame a father for being angry, can you?"

"No, you can't, but his daughter was sixteen at the time. Sex with a willing sixteen-year-old isn't considered much of a crime." Retelling Bill Hartley's story had created an opening, a crack in the door of Claire's past, a chance to tell her own story. The wrought iron table was too public a place, but it was the place Claire had chosen for this conversation. "I have to get back to work," she said, finishing her coffee.

"Before you go, I'm curious about one thing," Celia responded. "From what you told me it sounds like Edward Girard put his work before the people in his life. Is the work worth it?"

Claire might live to be a hundred and never be able to answer that question. "The deaths are horrible. The work is magnificent. That's all I can say."

While she waited for the detective to return her call, Claire worried that Owen would think she'd intruded on the APD's turf. Her previous attitude had been territorial. She'd made it clear she considered damaged books to be Claire's only legitimate involvement. But Maia's death was the only death Claire had to think about. She cared more than the APD did. Detective Owen ought to be pleased, at least, that she'd identified the victim.

Owen surprised Claire by showing up at her office without bothering to announce her presence at the information desk. Claire was engrossed in a computer search when she looked up and saw the detective standing in the doorway. Her hair seemed to be pulled up even tighter than usual, exaggerating the slant of her feral eyes.

"Am I interrupting you?" Owen asked. "I happened to be in the neighborhood."

"No," Claire replied, thinking Owen might have been deliberately trying to catch her off guard.

"Mind if I sit?" Owen sat without waiting for a reply. "I've had calls from Edward Girard and Allana Bruno, and she referred me to Bill Hartley. You were busy. Now I've been busy."

Claire couldn't tell from her expression whether she was annoyed or amused or grateful that Claire had gotten involved. "I went to the celebration at Spiral Rocks, trying to learn more about the place. I showed Edward a photocopy of the painting and told him what I knew about Maia. One thing led to another," she said. "I called you as soon as I got back."

"Well, some good came of your trip. Edward believes he is the victim's father and that her real name is June Reid. He has agreed to come to Albuquerque and submit to a DNA test. It will be good for everyone to identify the victim and provide some closure. If Edward is the father, he has agreed to take care of the burial. He told me there are no living relatives on the mother's side."

"The mother died at the Rio Grand Gorge in Taos," Claire said.

"So I heard. Allana Bruno told me she has been trying to prosecute Damon Fitzgerald for criminal sexual penetration. Unless a victim younger than thirteen comes forward, it will be difficult to convict him. When June Reid made an appointment, Allana was optimistic that she would be her witness, but then June died in the storage room."

"Maybe someone was trying to prevent her from being a witness," Claire said. It was a thought that had taken shape on the drive back from Taos.

Detective Owen chose her words with care. "Maybe someone was, but we have no evidence of that. All we have is a young woman dying alone with her drug of choice."

"Did you talk to Linda Butler at the Downtown Gallery about the woman who bought the painting?"

"Yes, but we didn't get much information. The buyer paid cash. Linda Butler's description of her was generic. Bill Hartley told me he talked to the victim shortly before she died. He has agreed to come down here and talk to us further."

"When I talked to him, he was very angry. He could have frightened Maia."

"What father wouldn't be angry?" Owen asked, raising a hand to smooth back her hair.

"From Bill's description it sounds like it was Ansia who told him where to find Maia. Have you talked to her yet?"

"We interviewed her, but she wasn't very forthcoming. She didn't mention anyone had been looking for Maia."

"Was the interviewer a man or a woman?" Claire asked.

"A man."

"You might have gotten more with a female investigator. Maia told me Ansia hates men. I've seen her react to security as if men are the enemy. So many women end up on drugs and on the street because of sexual abuse. It was June Reid's story. Maybe it's Ansia's story, too."

"She did speak to Bill Hartley," Detective Owen pointed out.

"She told him Maia hung out in the public library. We don't know what else she said."

Owen smiled. "Maybe we should give you

a badge and let you do the interviewing. You were right about the abuse when it came to Maia. I'll give you credit for that. What made you so sure?"

"Her attitude, the name Maia, the myth of the seven sisters fleeing to the sky to get away from an abusive man, the painting."

Detective Owen focused the power of her cat's eyes on Claire until she felt that she was getting a full body scan, that the detective could see every ounce of calcium that had leached out of her bones, every pinhole in her story. It made Claire want to run, but to run was to admit weakness or guilt. She made herself sit still and submit to the scan.

"Were you relying on your intuition?" Owen asked.

"Maybe it was just sympathy. In some way I suppose Maia confided in me." It was as far as Claire was willing to go. Owen stared just long enough to suggest she knew Claire herself had experienced more than she was telling. It was another chance for Claire to speak and this time to a professional, but she said nothing about her own experience. June Reid was the victim here, not Claire Reynier. Claire had been wounded by her experience, but June was dead.

"Well, it was a good thing that she spoke to you," Detective Owen said. "Without your help we might never have identified her. June

Reid would have been buried in an anonymous pauper's grave."

By now Claire knew enough about June Reid to think she might have preferred an anonymous grave. "I'm glad you think I've been a help and not an annoyance," she said.

Detective Owen smiled as she stood up. "I didn't say you weren't a nuisance," she said, "only that you were also a help."

Later in the afternoon an enthusiastic Lawton Davis showed up at Claire's door. "Well, how was it?" he asked. "Did the moon come up where it was supposed to?"

"Exactly where it was supposed to," Claire said. "The monument is magnificent, both the spiral rocks and the chambers Edward has built there."

"Did lots of people come?"

"Lots. It felt like a tribal celebration."

"Did you talk to Edward?"

"Yes. He believes Maia is his daughter, whom he hasn't seen since she was an infant."

"Well, that would explain her interest in the illustration and in the stars, wouldn't it?" Lawton asked.

"It would," Claire said.

"I'm in a bit of a rush right now, but when we both have more time, you must tell me all about it. All right?"

"All right."

Lawton started to walk away, then turned and poked his head back in the door. “I have just one more question for now. Did you get to see the shadow of Venus?”

“Not exactly,” Claire said.

# Chapter Twenty

At the end of the day Claire was walking through the Great Hall when she came across a security guard she recognized.

"Have you seen Ansia in the library recently?" she asked him.

"Not since we dragged her kicking and screaming out of the Willard Reading Room," he said. "She'll be back as soon as it rains."

Claire handed him her card. "If you see her, would you tell her I'd like to talk to her?"

"Sure."

It wasn't the first invitation Claire had handed out for Ansia. The response so far had not been encouraging.

Instead of leaving through the rear door that led to the parking lot, she went out through the main entrance and walked across campus to Central, which was filled as always with students toting backpacks and talking on their cell phones. Lack of a cell phone could be considered a sign of a homeless person, although these days even homeless people might have them. But who did they talk to? Each other? Claire searched Central, then turned to the side streets named after more prestigious schools: Yale, Harvard, Cornell, Stanford. She didn't see any of the plastic bags, bedrolls, or piled-high shopping carts that branded the carrier as a person living on the edge of sanity. She glanced into the shabbier parked cars, but she didn't see Ansia. Street people seemed to appear and disappear according to their own inner compass and logic. Some days there were a lot of them. Some days there were none. It seemed that when she had no interest in finding Ansia, she showed up all the time, but now that Claire wanted to find her, she had disappeared. Claire was disturbed by her inability to locate Ansia and worried about her safety. How would she ever know if something had happened to her?

She walked back across the campus, got in her truck, and drove home to her house in the foothills. Nemesis was waiting at the door. She let him out, followed him into her backyard, and watched him begin a cursory evening hunt. Claire had never seen him actually catch anything. Nemesis wasn't a cat who left piles of feathers on her stoop or showed up with a lizard in his mouth. He was a house cat who liked to wander in the evening but come home at night to sleep in Claire's warm bed. His eyes didn't have a wild hunter's gleam, but his body wasn't overly plump and pampered, either. Nemesis was a middle-class cat who lacked extremes and contradictions.

While he rummaged under her rose bushes, Claire looked up and saw the setting sun light a sliver of a cloud, creating a long, thin shadow that slithered up the Sandias. She lived in the foothills at the edge of a wilderness area. It was a place where coyotes, foxes, deer, bears, rattlesnakes, bobcats, and mountain lions found their way into backyards. Her neighborhood association hired a Varmint Master to kill the snakes and chase away the wild animals. It still amazed Claire that she could live in a city yet be so close to the wild.

She left Nemesis to his chase, went inside, dialed information, and asked for the number of Sophie Roybal in Durango. She justified to herself her reasons for calling Sophie. She would want to know about the death of her friend June Reid, and how could Claire be sure that anyone had told her? There were things she and Sophie could say to each other that would be hard to say to anyone else. But how to open the deadbolt in that door? Claire didn't turn the lights on and her living room had a velvety darkness.

She dialed the number. The woman who answered the phone had a question in her voice. "Hello?"

"Could I speak to Sophie Roybal?"

"This is me."

"Sophie, my name is Claire Reynier. I work at Zimmerman Library at UNM."

"You're calling about June." Sophie's voice went flat.

"Yes."

"I already heard that she died. That you were in Taos asking about her."

"From Allana Bruno?"

"From a friend."

Claire had the sense that Sophie's door was swinging shut. She tried to insert the words that would keep it open. "I have a copy of a beautiful painting of you, June, Maureen, Rose, and other girls dancing in a circle."

"That was a long time ago," Sophie said.

"I feel terrible about June's death. Maybe if someone had sought her out and talked to her she could have been helped."

"Bill Hartley sought her out and that helped a lot, didn't it?"

"Did he talk to you?"

"He's been trying, but I won't go there. I'm out of Taos now. I have my own life to live."

"Do you ever come to Albuquerque? I'd like to talk to you if you do." Albuquerque was the nearest city to Durango. Durango residents came to town for a number of reasons — to go to the airport, to shop, to see a doctor.

"I get to Albuquerque sometimes," Sophie admitted. "I have family there. But honestly I want to forget all about Taos and June Reid."

Claire found some words to keep the door

open a crack. "There are things you can never forget. You can put them on the shelf and not think about them for years and years but you can never forget. Talking can help."

"I'll think about it," Sophie said.

Claire gave her her home and office numbers. Sophie said good-bye and hung up, leaving Claire with no sense of whether she would ever hear from her again. She sat on the sofa, imagining she could hear the moths in the darkness. That night she dreamed about girls in white dresses floating sinuously above a river like the painting Lisa Teague had created of Ansia.

She woke up in the morning remembering that she hadn't checked her personal E-mail since the day she left for Colorado; she'd had too many other things on her mind. Before she even made a cup of coffee she went into her office and turned on the computer. In her absence her mailbox had filled up with the flotsam and jetsam of the computer age, endless offers to enlarge her penis, reduce her debt, buy the drugs that would keep her forever young from an on-line pharmacy. She began to hit the DELETE key, thinking that if she didn't stay on top of it she would be buried by it. But then among the junk she found a gem, an answer from Pietro.

His news was sad. "Thank you for your E-mail, Clara," it said. "I am glad that we knew each other when we did and that I helped you that day in Venice. You will always be a very special person to me. I am sorry I did not answer sooner. My wife died last month. It has been difficult for me and my daughter, but we are coping as best we can. Yours always, Pietro."

In Claire's experience death came as a shock no matter how long it had been expected. She'd been right when she'd sensed there was a reason to get in touch with Pietro that went deeper than dreams of romance. There was a shared history. There was empathy. It was easy to feel it, but harder to put it into words.

"I am so sorry for you and your daughter," she wrote. "It must have been terrible for you to watch your wife die and for your daughter to lose her mother at such a young age. My heart goes out to both of you. Please call if ever you want to talk about it."

Now that she'd written to him, she once again had to face the problem of how to end her message. She could take the tame way out and copy his "yours always," but she took an emotional leap, closed with "Love, Clara" and clicked the SEND button before she was able to change her mind.

# Chapter Twenty-one

A few days later Jennifer Rule called to say that Edward Girard was coming to town and that she wanted to make an appointment for him to see Claire. As in their previous conversations, her manner was brisk and efficient. Although the last time Claire had seen Jennifer she was in Edward's kitchen dressed in jeans, she visualized her in a business suit in a slick office running the affairs of a busy executive rather than the affairs of a celestial artist. Claire was curious as to whether Jennifer traveled with Edward. Would she be coming to Albuquerque with him? Jennifer hung up before Claire could ask.

A number had shown up on caller ID but the name was Alltel Wireless, indicating Jennifer had called from a cell phone. The number didn't reveal whether she lived at Spiral Rocks or not. Much of the promotional work she did could be accomplished anywhere by E-mail, fax, or phone. Jennifer seemed too energetic and active to be content in such an isolated place, but she wouldn't have to live at Spiral Rocks to be Edward's lover. She could visit. They could travel together. Edward was a man who was likely to prefer a long-distance relationship, someone who would supply sex when he wanted it, stay out of the way when he didn't.

Claire knew other men who were willing to let a lover be a buffer and run the details of their lives. Jennifer appeared to be ten or twelve years younger than Edward, an age that was likely to appeal to him.

Jennifer's call reminded Claire that she hadn't checked the article in the Taos paper yet. She got on the Internet, went to the paper's Web site, signed on as a user, and agreed to pay the price it cost to look at old news. She searched through the archives until she found the article about Veronica Reid's death, which didn't speculate as to whether the death was deliberate or accidental. There was no mention of a suicide note. Veronica left behind a daughter named June Reid who lived in Taos. The article differed from Edward's account in the detail of where Veronica died. It confirmed Bill Hartley's story that Veronica had fallen or leapt from Buffalo Point, not from the bridge. It was tempting to attribute Edward's misstatement to dishonesty or deviousness, but it was also possible that Edward had forgotten what he had read. He was old enough and distracted enough to muddle the past.

What Claire could not explain or understand was why he hadn't contacted his daughter when he heard her mother had died. If his daughter had sent him the article, his lack of a response could be considered another nail in the coffin of a father's indifference. Spiral Rocks was remote in spirit but only a few hours' drive from Taos. It was possible that all Edward Girard knew of the events in Taos was the newspaper article. Not wanting to find out more showed an extreme lack of curiosity, but Edward also showed an extreme absorption in his work. On the other hand he might have known more and not have wanted to admit it, Claire thought. The web of friends and gossip she had uncovered so far had reached as far away as Durango. Why not to Spiral Rocks? Claire could ask Edward about the bridge when she saw him, but it would be harder to ask about the events in Taos and why he hadn't gotten in touch with his only child.

Before she left the Internet, she did a search on Edward Girard's name. She didn't find a Web site for him, but she found hundreds of articles about him and his work. She only had time to skim, but every one she glanced at was full of praise for the work of Edward Girard.

The meeting was arranged for Claire's office at CSWR. When Edward arrived he gave his name at the Information Desk and Claire walked out to meet him. Wanting to show him the Willard Reading Room where she'd last seen his daughter, she led him into the Great Hall. Edward looked up at the high ceilings with row after row of carved vigas.

"I suppose you could say that John Gaw Meem reinvented the pueblo with all these vigas and corbels," he said. "I know other architects criticize him for not being more creative, but this building works as a library. In a way it's a cathedral of learning. Students like to study here, don't they?"

"Yes," Claire said. "And it's a pleasure to work here, too."

Edward wore hiking boots, faded jeans, and an equally faded shirt, the same way he had dressed at Spiral Rocks, but he seemed different here. At Spiral Rocks he was master of all he surveyed and at ease. Here he had the edgy alert quality of a wild animal in an alien environment, seeing all, hearing all, smelling all. Unlike the students who walked around with their ears glued to their cell phones, oblivious of their surroundings, Edward was acutely aware of where he was. He held his head high. His eyes circled the Great Hall. He had the ripe odor of a hiker who has spent days out on the trail.

Claire showed him the Willard Reading Room with its interior windows that faced the hall and exterior windows that faced the cactus garden. Today it was full of light and space and nearly devoid of people. She told

Edward about her encounter with June and how packed the room had been that day.

"I'm not comfortable in rooms full of people myself," he said. "The Navajo always leave a line to the edge of their weavings as a way out. An open door could have the same effect. I wonder if June came to Zimmerman to die because she admired the building. This would be a good place to die."

"She died in a storage room in the basement. It didn't have high ceilings and vigas and light," Claire said. She couldn't tell a father it did have dirt and roaches. "Would you like to see it?"

"No." Edward's answer was short and definite. "I'd prefer to go outside. Could we talk there?"

"All right," Claire said.

They went outside and sat down on a bench beside the duck pond, where the reflection of the library's tower rippled across the water. Sitting next to Edward on the bench brought his wild animal smell closer. Claire knew what smells revealed among animals — fear, submission, aggression. She didn't smell fear or aggression on Edward. She smelled an unease that she couldn't identify.

"Most of the library works, but I don't like that tower. It's supposed to be reaching for the sky, but it's squat and dumpy." Edward threw a rock in the pond, causing the tower's reflection to ripple and lengthen. "There. That's better," he said.

"I spoke to June here," Claire told him. "It was evening and she pointed out the Venus-Jupiter conjunction. This is where she told me: 'Venus is brighter than most people know, so bright it casts a shadow. It's visible in the daytime to those who have eyes to see.' "

"That sounds like something a daughter of mine would say," Edward replied. "It's interesting, isn't it, how she took after both me and her mother? It makes sense with her mother, since Veronica raised her, but with me it has to be genetic. What other explanation is there for her interest in art and in Venus?"

"That she knew all about you and followed your career." It seemed obvious to Claire. "Anyone who visits a library has access to the Internet. There's lots of information about your work on-line — Spiral Rocks, the Maximum Moon, the Venus Chamber, can all be found on the Internet."

"Can they?" Edward was indifferent. "I never look. I leave all that to Jennifer."

"If June tried to contact you, if she had wanted to come to the celebration, would she have gotten Jennifer?"

"Most likely. If I answered the phone, I'd never get anything done."

"Would Jennifer have connected her to you or brushed her off?"

"That would depend on what June said. You'd have to ask Jennifer. She's talking to the galleries in Santa Fe today, trying to promote my smaller installations. I gave a sample of my saliva to the police this morning so they'll know for sure whether June is my daughter. Once they establish that, they can release the body. If she is my daughter, I want to take her back to Spiral Rocks and bury her there. Maybe near the Venus Chamber."

"Where was Veronica buried? Do you know?"

"Somewhere in Taos, I suppose." He slouched on the bench and stretched his long legs out in front of him.

"She died near Buffalo Point, not at the Taos Gorge Bridge. I found the article about her that appeared in the paper."

"What did I say? The bridge? Maybe that's how I visualized it in my mind. Does it really matter whether it was the bridge or the point? She died in the Rio Grande Gorge."

"It could make a difference. In some ways her death resembles June's. They might be suicides. Then again they might not," Claire said, trying to pass her suspicions on to Edward.

He refused to accept them. "Of course they were suicides," he said, sitting up straight on the bench and tossing his hair back over his shoulder. "When I was at the police station this morning, no one suggested anything other than a woman in trouble alone with her drugs."

Claire moved on. "I talked to Sophie Roybal, another young woman who was abused by Damon Fitzgerald. She lives in Durango, yet she knew about June's death. She knew I'd been to Taos. There's a strong network among the people who lived in the Cave Commune."

"It's not a network, it's a web, and Damon Fitzgerald is the spider. I have no connection to those people." Edward threw another rock in the pond. It landed near a startled duck that responded by quacking and flapping its wings. "I don't want anything to do with that untalented predator, but I'd like to meet the artist who painted June while I am in town. Can you arrange it?"

"I'll call her. How long are you staying?"

"Through tomorrow. I'll give you my cell phone number. There's a sculpture around here somewhere called *The Center of the Universe*. Have you got the time to show it to me?"

Claire made the time and they walked along the side of Smith Plaza that was landscaped with rosemary bushes. Edward snapped off a twig and sniffed it as they walked by. The strength of his own wild animal odor came and went depending on proximity. In *The Center of the Universe* two large metal shapes connected in a cross tall enough to walk through. Most people did it as quickly as possible. It resembled a sterile metal tunnel, a dead zone devoid of any sense of feeling or life. The only escape was an opening in the top revealing a patch of blue sky. Claire couldn't imagine a sculpture more different from the sinuous, evocative chambers Edward had created at Spiral Rocks. There she felt stimulated and sheltered at the same time. Here she felt oppressed.

Edward stopped in the middle of *The Center of the Universe*, looked up, and stared with longing at the sky as if he already missed being on the mesa with his stars and his rocks. As a student walked through the sculpture, her cell phone rang.

"Hey, what's up?" she said without breaking stride.

Edward laughed. "Whatever happened to 'be here now'? I hope the artist was being ironic when he named this piece."

"I'd like to think so," Claire said.

"I'll let you know when the DNA results come back. I'm going to Los Angeles to finish an installation at MOCA, the Museum of Contemporary Art, next month. Maybe I can recover June's body on my way back. I'd like to do it all in one trip if possible. I've gotten so I hate to be away from Spiral Rocks. It's the center of my universe."

"It's a good one," Claire said.

She left Edward on the far side of the sculpture, walked back to her office, and called Lisa Teague to tell her about Edward's interest.

"Edward Girard is Maia's father?" Lisa asked. "Oh, my God. How did such a wonderful artist's daughter end up homeless on the street?"

"He hasn't seen her since she was an infant."

"You'd think someone as talented as Edward Girard would stay in touch with his own daughter. Wouldn't he want to see what kind of talent she had? I love his work."

"Have you been to Spiral Rocks?" Claire asked.

"I wish. I saw one of his smaller installations in Denver."

"Spiral Rocks is a magnificent place. I went there for the Maximum Moon celebration, and I showed Edward a copy of *Summertime*. He admired it very much and said he would like to meet you."

"Just say where and when."

"I'll give him your number. You should be hearing from him or the publicist who arranges everything for him. Her name is Jennifer Rule. I'm still trying to track down the woman who bought the original of *Summertime*. You haven't heard any more about her, have you?"

"No," Lisa said. "To tell you the truth I'd rather not know who buys my paintings. Before I take them to the shelter or the gallery I hold a little ceremony and say good-bye. It's like sending a child off to school. They don't belong to me anymore. They belong to . . . whoever. You should have one yourself."

"I should," Claire agreed.

"When I paint one that's just right for you, I'll let you know."

"Thanks," Claire said.

# Chapter Twenty-two

A notecard came in the mail from Lisa Teague with a replica of a painting that was unmistakably hers on the front. A woman in pink balanced very carefully on a tightrope. She was in the precarious situation of a homeless person, but her face was fresh and clean and full of hope. Claire liked it — she liked all of Lisa's paintings she'd seen — but this wasn't the one she wanted to own.

"Hi," the note read. "This is a computer-generated image of a painting that's still available, if you're interested. It was great to meet Edward Girard. Things might have ended up very differently if Maia had only known her father. He had nice things to say about my work and bought three paintings. Jennifer, his publicist, wants to show them to gallery owners she knows in Santa Fe. Thanks so much for telling Edward about me. Lisa."

Claire called to thank her for the note.

"Did you like that painting?" Lisa asked. "The model is doing well at the moment. She's out of the shelter, studying at TVI. A rare success story."

"I like it," Claire said. "But I don't think

it's the one I'm looking for. I'll know it when I see it."

"I'm sure you will. Edward Girard was great, very encouraging. I hope he's not being so kind because he feels guilty about his own daughter."

"You do exceptional work," Claire said. "Edward recognizes that."

"He says I should forget about social work, forget about school, forget about having anything to fall back on, and just paint." She laughed. "That also means forget about paying the rent, forget about getting along with my mother."

"That's what it takes to be an artist."

"It's what Edward did. He's a genius. His work will last, but his daughter posed for one of my paintings. She died alone of a drug overdose. To put art first isn't an easy decision."

Claire believed that it wasn't a matter of making a decision, that for artists like Edward there was no choice. If Lisa saw a fork in the road, she might never fulfill her potential as an artist. On the other hand she would be a dutiful daughter. She might become a mother.

"Did you meet Jennifer?" Claire asked her.

"Yes."

"What did you think of her?"

"She came to my studio, but she wasn't thrilled by Central. She acted like she was protecting the famous artist from the riffraff, but I guess Edward needs that. I paint riffraff myself so I have to be in touch with them. Jennifer liked my work and she has a lot of connections."

What kind of a connection does she have with Edward? Claire wanted to ask. Is she sleeping with him? How far would she go to protect him? She left those questions locked in the closet and said good-bye to Lisa.

Claire was walking down the library steps on her way to the Humanities Building when a woman approached her. She was about Claire's height but broader and more muscular. Her blond hair was pulled back in a ponytail, making her look almost young enough to be an undergraduate. She had an undergraduate's way of speaking in italics and ending sentences with a question mark that should have ended in a period.

"Claire Reynier?" the woman asked.

"Yes?" Claire answered, trying unsuccessfully to place her.

"My name is Bettina Hartley. You met my husband, Bill? In Taos?"

"That's right. I met him on the path near the Rio Grande Gorge Bridge," Claire said. "How did you know who I was?"

"Bill described you and told me where you worked. He's a good observer."

Claire thought that everyone in Taos knew

far too much about everyone else. One reason she didn't want to live in a small town was that she valued her privacy. It unnerved her to think that all she had done was visit Taos and now people she'd never met could identify her.

"Bill said you left a message on our answering machine?"

"Yes. I was hoping to talk to him while he was in Albuquerque."

"He's with the police department now and he asked me to come over and visit with you. Bill didn't scare you at the gorge, I hope," Bettina said.

"It was unnerving to meet a man there, but I wouldn't say that he scared me."

"Bill can be kind of intense at times, but he's a good man, very devoted to me and our daughter, Rose."

"You look so young to have a twenty-year-old daughter," Claire said.

Bettina smiled at the compliment. "Bill said you knew June?"

"I met her in the library a couple of times. I wouldn't say that I knew her."

"June was a sweet child, and smart, too. It's just a shame what happened to her. To be abused by Damon Fitzgerald, then to lose her mother, and finally to die of an overdose at such a young age." She shivered although the temperature was at least ninety degrees.

Claire agreed that those events were all terrible.

"Did June tell you about her meeting with Bill? I hope he didn't frighten her when he talked to her."

Claire couldn't help noticing that this was the second time in a very brief conversation that Bettina Hartley had hoped her husband hadn't frightened a vulnerable woman. Although the only information Claire had about Bill's meeting with June came from Bill himself, it was tempting to answer "Actually, he scared the hell out of June" just to see what kind of a reaction that would get from Bettina, but that was a lie and lying was a line Claire wasn't ready to cross.

"He told me the librarian at the Main Library on Copper asked him to leave," Claire said. "I gather he raised his voice, which could be intimidating to someone as fragile as June."

"Well, sometimes he loses his temper and does raise his voice, but that's as far as it ever goes. Really. Bill is very strong, of course; he won an Iron Man Triathlon last year, but he would never *hurt* anyone." Bettina tugged the leather strap of her shoulder bag for emphasis. "I know the police will understand that when they talk to him."

"I would think if he was going to hurt anyone, it would be Damon Fitzgerald," Claire said.

"He gets angry whenever he sees Damon and punches the steering wheel, but that's the only way he expresses it. I'm sure if Bill got into a physical fight with Damon, he would win. But Bill would never resort to physical violence. Never."

Claire wondered whether Bettina meant physical violence with a man or with anybody. Was Bill Hartley a man who had a taboo about not fighting other men but was unable to control himself when it came to women? Had Bill ever hurt Bettina or his own daughter? Why had Bettina brought up the subject of her husband's temper? "Bill seemed very upset by Damon's affair with your daughter," Claire said.

"Rose always was a daddy's girl," Bettina replied. "She could do no wrong in her father's eyes. He puts her on a pedestal, and of course it was terrible for Damon to get involved with her. But she was sixteen. She wasn't a child. Bill forgets that we were sixteen when we got together and only eighteen when Rose was born. She'll get over Damon. It's good for her to be out of Taos and away from all the gossip, but we miss her. We're a close family. Bill's hope is that Damon will be put in prison and then Rose will want to come back home."

"I was told that people were very angry with Veronica about June," Claire said.

"*Very* angry." Bettina swung her ponytail

for emphasis. "She should have protected her daughter. Absolutely. Do you think that June could have inherited a suicidal tendency from her mother? Is that possible?"

"June's father thinks so," Claire said.

"That's good, isn't it? I mean better that than someone else harmed June."

"The police have found no evidence to support that," Claire said.

"It's very sad that June died. Very sad. Now it looks like the most Damon Fitzgerald will ever get is a slap on the wrist."

"Unless he does it again."

"Do you think he will in Taos with everybody watching their daughters now and watching him?"

Claire recalled a sexual offender who came to New Mexico after serving his prison sentence but was hounded and driven from town to town, never being allowed to stay in one place long enough to cause any harm. She couldn't imagine that happening to Damon Fitzgerald. He was too shrewd, too cunning, too capable of turning on the charm when he had to. "I don't know," Claire said.

"Well, I don't want to take up any more of your time," Bettina said, giving Claire's hand a little pat. "I just thought I'd stop by and visit for a while while Bill was busy with the APD. You've been very helpful. Thank you so much."

Claire watched Bettina walk away. A decisive swish of the ponytail seemed to imply she thought this meeting had accomplished something. But what? was Claire's question. Bettina had obviously been looking for information about Bill's meetings with Claire and with June. Did she fear he'd been violent or threatening? Bettina was likely to know more about her husband's capacity for violence than anyone else, but how much of that knowledge would she share? Bettina struck Claire as one of those women with a cheerful, self-effacing manner who tries to make things better but ends up making them worse, which could indicate a subconscious desire to mess things up. If there had been any incidents of domestic violence in the Hartley household, Allana Bruno would know about it, unless the violence had never been reported.

Claire went back to her office, wondering whether Bill knew about Bettina's visit. She waited all afternoon to see if he would show up or call himself, but he never did.

# Chapter Twenty-three

The following day Claire took advantage of her lunch hour to drive downtown to Copper to the main branch of the public library. She parked on the corner of Sixth Street in front of a parking meter painted with art deco swirls. A homeless man had parked his shopping cart piled high with clothes and bedrolls beside the library. Claire was glad to see that he was engrossed in a book.

She walked around the corner and went through the library's main entrance. There was fluorescent lighting in this library and red plastic chairs at laminated tables. Security guards in blue windbreakers were strategically placed. This library had none of the charm of Zimmerman and it seemed strange to Claire that Maia would hang out here. It was possible she got sick of being in the same place all the time or maybe being at Zimmerman 24/7 made her too easy to find.

Before she left her office Claire did her homework and learned that the librarian she needed to talk to was named Dorothy Bronwin. She took the elevator to the second floor and went through the glass door marked ADMINISTRATIVE TECHNICAL SERVICES. Dorothy was in her office clicking away at her keyboard. Claire tapped on the open door and Dorothy looked up.

"May I come in? I'm Claire Reynier."

Dorothy didn't stand up and say "Welcome," but she didn't say "Go away, I'm busy," either, so Claire stepped into the office. "I work at the Center for Southwest Research at UNM." Claire did not follow Bettina's example and add a question mark to the end of her sentence. She was who she was, even though she knew that might cause resentment here. Public librarians tended to think of university librarians as humorless and arrogant intellectuals. University librarians worked in a highly competitive atmosphere where they were forced to act humble until they were granted tenure and earned the right be as arrogant as everyone else. Claire had been in academia long enough to know how often arrogance masked insecurity.

"Dorothy Bronwin," the librarian said. Her bright red lipstick bled into the cracks around her mouth. Her hair was too black to be real. She didn't get up from her desk, so it was hard for Claire to judge how tall she was, although the size of her upper body indicated she was a large woman. There wasn't an uncluttered surface in the office to sit on, which left Claire standing and towering over Dorothy, not a position she wanted to be in.

"Did you ever encounter a homeless

woman who called herself Maia and spent some time here?" Claire asked Dorothy.

"That's the woman who died in the basement of Zimmerman?"

"Yes."

"She came here sometimes. She was quiet and kept to herself."

"Was there some kind of altercation with a man a couple of weeks ago?"

"I wouldn't say it was an altercation — more of an argument." Dorothy swung around in her desk chair to face Claire. "How did you know about that?"

"The man involved told me. His name is Bill Hartley and he's a ski instructor in Taos."

"Did he say it was an altercation?"

"Not really. He said he raised his voice and was asked to leave."

"That's right." Dorothy put her elbows on her desk. "Well, if he told you all about it, then what can I do for you?"

"I don't know that he did tell me all about it," Claire said.

"Maia died of an overdose in Zimmerman, right?"

"Apparently."

"Does it matter now what happened here?"

"It might." Dorothy was making her work for every tidbit of information. Claire believed that was the price she paid for being a university librarian. It was annoying but she felt she had to continue.

"The man raised his voice. A security guard asked him to be quiet or leave. He apologized and left, but then he came back and the argument started all over again. The guard was new to the job and she called me. This sort of disruption happens all the time here."

"It happens at Zimmerman, too," Claire said.

"Well, you have more security at Zimmerman. Here we have a couple of guards and we have me." Dorothy laughed. "I will say that this man was a better class of troublemaker than we usually get. He was clean, sober, sane. I thought he might be someone from Maia's past. When I told him I would have to call the police if he didn't leave, he apologized and left. That was the end of it. I never saw him again."

"What were they arguing about?"

"He was telling her there was something she had to do. No matter how hard it was, she had to do it for the sake of the other girls. He was very insistent."

"Was Maia afraid of him?"

"I don't know that she was afraid, but she certainly wasn't happy about the encounter. She was in tears when he left. What was it that he wanted her to do? Do you know?"

"Go back to Taos and testify against a man who abused her when she was twelve years old."

"No wonder she was in tears. Is the abuse what put her on the street?"

"I believe it was."

"Figures." Dorothy's fingers returned to her keyboard, skirting the edge as if they were anxious to continue typing. "I hope she testified before she died and put the son of a bitch away."

"She called the Taos County DA and agreed to talk to her, but she died before she ever got to Taos."

"Well, that makes her death even sadder, doesn't it? Why did this Bill Hartley get involved?"

"His daughter had sex with the same man but she was too old for it to be a prosecutable offense. Maia was Bill's best hope of putting the abuser in prison."

"He'll probably do it again," Dorothy sighed. "They always do."

"Did Maia come back to the library after that encounter?"

"You know, I don't remember seeing her, but homeless people come and go and we don't pay much attention to them until something bad happens, do we?"

"I'm afraid not," Claire said. "Do you ever see Ansia here?"

"She used to come to the library, but she caused too much trouble. She has wild mood swings. She'd fall asleep at a table, snore, and disturb everybody, then she'd wake up and become belligerent. And the smell! Whew!" Dorothy held her nose. "We had to get tough and not let her in. I haven't seen her for some time."

Claire handed Dorothy her card. "If you do see her, would you tell her I'd like to talk to her?"

"Sure. You may not want to take any advice from me," Dorothy said, pushing herself out of her chair and standing up. She wasn't any taller than Claire was. It was her bulldog attitude, not her size, that gave her the power to evict the troublemakers. "But here it is. It's not a good idea to start caring about drug addicts and street people who have gone over the edge. They'll break your heart every damn time."

"I'll remember that," Claire said.

Before she left the library she walked around the second floor, where the periodicals were kept. There were enough magazines on display here to fill dozens of waiting rooms. She wouldn't mind spending an afternoon on this floor escaping through magazines. She saw a large window on the far side of the room facing a parking garage. The garage's blank wall was decorated with large Xs painted in primary colors. Two chairs sat in the window facing out. Claire believed that was where Maia would have wanted to sit when she came to the main library.

★ ★ ★

On the drive back through downtown Claire thought about what had transpired between Bill Hartley and Maia. It could have been fear of him or returning to Taos that had caused her to OD. Maia had called Allana Bruno and said she would meet with her. Of all the people Claire had spoken to regarding Maia, the one with the most credibility was Allana Bruno. Although she might not have told her everything, Claire believed what she had said. But something more ominous might have happened, something Allana Bruno didn't know about, between the time Maia made the decision to go to Taos and the time she took the China White.

# Chapter Twenty-four

On Monday Sophie Roybal surprised Claire by calling to say she was in town for a few hours. It was noon and she asked if Claire wanted to meet her for lunch. The timing of the call made Claire suspect that Sophie was going through the motions, all the while hoping Claire would be unavailable.

But she was available. "Where can we meet?" Claire asked.

"Outside the bookstore?" Sophie said. "I need to buy a textbook and I can get a used copy there."

"How will I know you?"

"I have long black hair," Sophie said.

Long black hair wouldn't distinguish anyone at UNM, but Claire let that go by, hoping she'd find some other way to identify Sophie.

She put a copy of *Summertime* in a folder and held it under her arm as she stood waiting outside the bookstore. As soon as Sophie came through the inner door with a bookstore bag in her hand, Claire knew who she was. Sophie was defined by her hair, a waterfall of thick black curls that tumbled down her back. It was hair men would want to smell, touch, bury their faces in. Sophie's full hair was an attention-getting contrast to her slender, graceful figure. She wore a thigh-length skirt that emphasized her slenderness. It was easy enough to imagine strangers approaching Sophie Roybal and telling her she looked beautiful. She moved with the reserved self-assurance of a woman who was accustomed to admiration but remained indifferent to it. Claire began to think she'd gotten the wrong impression about Sophie Roybal; there was nothing in her manner or appearance to suggest this confident young woman had ever been abused.

It wasn't until she walked up close that Claire saw any sign of "a girl who." Sophie's features and complexion were perfect. She had nothing to emphasize or conceal. Even though she needed no makeup, she wore far too much — mauve eye shadow, purplish lipstick outlined in an almost black shade, blush that was a bright slash on her cheeks. It reminded Claire of the overdone clown makeup in Lisa Teague's paintings.

"Are you Sophie?" she asked.

"I am."

"I'm Claire Reynier."

"Hi," Sophie said.

"Did you find the textbook you wanted?"

"Yes." Sophie glanced at her watch. "How about the Olympia Café for lunch? It's right across the street."

The Olympia Café was crowded and noisy at lunchtime and Claire avoided going there, but she agreed. They ordered gyros at the counter, found a booth to sit in, and waited for their number to come up. A man stood at the counter yelling out numbers as the orders were filled, not necessarily in numerical order: sixty-four, fifty-eight, sixty-seven. Conversation with Sophie was difficult enough without the numerical interjections.

"June called herself Maia when she was in Albuquerque," Claire said, trying to get a conversation going.

"Oh yeah?" Sophie replied.

Two academics in the adjacent booth argued about physics. It seemed far too complicated to try to explain why June called herself Maia in the noise and confusion of the Olympia Café, far too confusing to introduce *Summertime* here. "Did you ever see her when you came to town?" Claire asked.

"No. I didn't even know she was here until I heard she had died."

"Sixty-six," the owner yelled.

Claire tried again. "I met June twice, once at a reading at the library, once beside the duck pond. She talked me to about the stars." Claire paused. "She told me I looked beautiful."

Sophie smiled. "She used to tell me that I looked beautiful, too. You could tell her she was pretty forever, but she would never believe it."

"Did you live at the commune?"

"For a while."

"What do you do in Durango?" Claire asked.

"I'm getting a degree in anthropology at Fort Lewis College."

"That's good."

"It beats hanging out in Taos," Sophie said.

"Seventy-two," the man called. "Seventy-four."

"That's my number." Sophie jumped up and went to get her gyro. Heads turned as she walked through the restaurant. Heads turned again as she walked back. There was a pause in the beat of the argument in the adjacent booth. Igniting the fantasies of men was the blessing of being young and beautiful, but it was also the curse, Claire thought. She was struck by the difference in the demeanor of the dramatic Sophie and the subdued June who had dressed and acted as if she wanted to disappear. June hid her essence behind the faded clothes of a homeless person while Sophie hid behind her beauty.

"I brought your order, too," she said, putting both gyros on the table.

"Thanks," Claire said.

Eating made conversation even more difficult. Claire gave up and concentrated on her gyro. When Sophie finished she took out a compact and lipstick, redid her lips, then closed the compact with a decisive click.

"Ready?" she asked Claire.

"Ready," Claire said.

As they got up and walked through the restaurant and out the door Claire despaired of accomplishing anything. Had Sophie come all the way from Durango to say nothing? There had to be something she was willing to reveal, but Claire didn't know how to get her to open up.

They stood on Central. Sophie extended her hand and said, "Nice meeting you."

The picture of the girls was still in the folder under Claire's arm, unseen by Sophie. It was about to become the perfunctory end to a perfunctory meeting when a homeless woman walked down Central pulling her belongings behind her in a shopping cart. She stopped and stared into a parked car's side-view mirror, rearranging her hair.

"Addicts look into car mirrors to find veins in their eyeballs that they can use to shoot up," Claire said. It was a grim fact of street life that she had learned from Detective Owen and one way to get Sophie's attention.

Sophie cringed.

"That's how June ended up," Claire continued. "On the street. On drugs. Dead in a storage room in the library's basement."

Sophie's eyes flashed. "Well, you can blame her mother and Damon Fitzgerald for that.

Her mother should have kept that man away from June."

"We need to talk somewhere, Sophie. In private." Claire had been struggling to find a secluded place to talk; there weren't many at UNM. But then she had an inspiration. "I know just the place." She switched into mother mode, using a tone of voice that would tolerate no hesitation or excuses from a woman young enough to be her daughter. "Come with me."

Sophie might have been waiting for a firm hand. She didn't give Claire an argument, following her across Central and into the Center for the Arts. Claire was hoping the Rodey Theatre would be open and empty and was relieved to find that it was. Popejoy Hall was too large for an intimate conversation, Theatre X was too far away in the basement, but Rodey was nearby and it happened to be available. Nothing was in rehearsal at the moment. They sat down in seats in the back row facing the empty stage. Sophie put her knees up against the back of the seat in front of her. Claire's imagination filled the stage with images of twinkling stars and girls dancing in summer dresses.

"Tell me what happened in Taos," she said. "It's important to know how and why June died."

Sophie wrapped a black curl around her finger and gave it a tug. "What happened is that June slept with Damon Fitzgerald, her mother's lover."

"It's hard for me to understand why she would do such a thing."

"It wouldn't be so hard if you had been there. Veronica had her own problems and she ignored June. Maybe June was trying to get her attention or get even, or maybe she was just young and naïve enough to fall for Damon. He was charismatic and had a lot of power in Cave Commune. It meant a girl was special when Damon singled her out, but he went too far when he got involved with June. The commune fell apart after that. Later Veronica was found dead in the Rio Grande Gorge. Put it all together and you can understand why June died."

"Did Veronica kill herself?"

"Who knows? Her body was so mangled when it was found, no one will ever know. She could have been pushed over the edge. People at the commune blamed Veronica for what happened. Some of them were very angry."

"Shouldn't Damon be the one to take the blame?"

"Of course, but Veronica was dispensable. Damon wasn't. It was convenient to blame her. Damon was the pied piper. There were people at Cave Commune with no lives of their own who would have followed him anywhere. One time we all went rafting in the

Rio Grande and Damon jumped out of the raft into the river. The water was snowmelt and freezing cold but everybody followed him into it like mice. Damon was good-looking and charming. Then he discovered the drug Ecstasy. When he started handing that out it made him irresistible. I had support from my family. I got over it. June didn't."

"How old were you?"

"Fourteen. Old enough to know better."

"Young enough for it to be criminal sexual penetration, which is a felony."

"But not a first-degree felony. Trust me, I've been through all this with Allana Bruno. June was the only one young enough for it to be a first-degree felony. For the rest of us time will eventually run out. But as long as June was alive and willing to testify, Damon could have been prosecuted. There is no statute of limitations when you have sex with a twelve-year-old."

The darkness of the theater and Sophie's openness made it possible for Claire to say the words she had kept under lock and key for so long. "Twelve is a dangerous age, old enough to attract predators, young enough to be defenseless. I was molested by a friend's father at that age."

Sophie let go of her hair and the curl bounced over her shoulder. "Women tell me stories like that all the time once they find out about me and Damon. Some men — relatives, uncles, friends, strangers, whatever — can't keep their hands off young women. With men like that, the more forbidden and dangerous the act, the more they are turned on by it. I'm sorry for your friend. I'm sorry for you. I'm sorry for all of us. But you only get one life and you can't let the Damon Fitzgeralds ruin it." Sophie dropped her feet to the floor and sat up straight in her chair. "One thing you can count on is that I'm going to graduate from school. I'm not going to die homeless and drugged out like June did. I may be all Allana Bruno has left now to try to make a case against Damon before the statute of limitations runs out. But do you know what it would be like to stand up in court, face the guy who did it, and tell the whole world about it? Did you do that?"

"No. I couldn't bear to hurt my friend and my family. I never even told my parents."

"I suppose you thought you did something to encourage the guy, right?"

"I was afraid that I had."

Sophie stared at the empty stage. "My family lives in Taos. Why should I have to go to court and embarrass them? I'm doing well in school. I have a life. I have a boyfriend. Why go back to Taos and wreck it all? It's not even a first-degree felony in my case. Look at me. You know the defense lawyer is going to say that I seduced Damon. And what would he get even if he was convicted?

A couple of months in the state pen?" She turned toward Claire and said softly, "Tell me this. Would you testify if you had to do it all over again?"

"I don't know. I'll always be sorry that I did nothing to stop the man from molesting or raping other girls. I know now that abusers don't stop until they are caught."

"Sooner or later they get too old for it, don't they?" Sophie's voice had a hopeful tone.

"But it's never soon enough. You could help make sure there were no more Junes for Damon Fitzgerald."

"Only for the time that he's in prison, if he even goes to prison. I could also become another June. I could be risking more than my happiness and my reputation by testifying. I could be risking my life."

"Do you think someone killed June?"

"I don't know."

"How could that be possible? The police said her prints were the only ones on the needle."

Sophie stared at the blank stage and said, "Damon would be the logical person, I suppose, but I never saw him be violent. He's the kind of man who kills with a kiss. Bill Hartley is very angry. June could have met someone in Albuquerque who wanted to harm her, I guess."

"A woman bought the original of the

painting of June and the other girls and paid cash for it. I'd like to find out who she is."

"Show me your copy," Sophie said. "I'm ready to look at it now."

Claire took *Summertime* out of its folder and handed it to her. Sophie stared at the image. "We were so young then," she said, "so innocent, so dumb. And then the caveman came out of the cave. Damon ruled at Cave Commune. It went to his head and he thought he could get away with anything he wanted to. In a way I guess he did."

"I met him," Claire said. "I went to his house in Taos."

"It's not his house," Sophie said. "It belongs to Sharon Miller. It was her vacation getaway in Taos and then she met Damon, moved to town, took him in, and started supporting him. She inherited the bucks. Sharon never earned a penny in her life. She tried to pursue a creative career when she was younger but she didn't get anywhere. So she made Damon her career. When he finds some other way to support himself he'll break her heart just like he's broken everyone else's in his life. I used to think you'd have to be fourteen years old to fall for Damon, but there was Veronica and now there's Sharon. There's always a woman willing to be a fool for a good-looking man. What did you think of him?"

"That he was a ladies' man and not much of an architect."

"Every time he tried for a commission and didn't get it, he slept with someone else. The troubles at the commune began when Damon lost out on the Center of Light Chapel. It was the largest church ever built in Taos, a major commission that would have put his name on the map. The congregation was open to new ideas. They really wanted to use a Taos architect and Damon expected to be chosen, but the committee dissed his design."

"Did he sleep with all the girls in the painting?"

"The only ones I know for sure were me and June and Bill Hartley's daughter, Rose. Part of Damon's act was to play us off against each other, to get the girls competing for his favors."

"What about Maureen Prescott? Did she sleep with Damon, too? Could he be the father of her baby?"

"Maureen claims Tommy Courier is the father and he never denied it. The baby looks like Tommy. I don't know if Maureen slept with Damon. Maybe June knew something I didn't when she had that picture painted. If she did sleep with Damon, Nancy, Maureen's mother, would never let her talk about it. Nancy still idolizes Damon. She believed all of his bullshit and was totally committed to the commune. They're still living there, aren't they?"

"That's where I met them. Was it Maureen

who told you about me?"

"Yeah. It was her. We've stayed friends."

Sophie put the picture back in the folder. "When the person who was responsible for June's death is locked up, that's when I'll be willing to testify against Damon Fitzgerald."

"That's unlikely to happen. The police think June's death was either an accidental or a suicidal overdose. They believe the only criminal was the person who sold her China White."

"Then I'll never testify. I have to go. Can I keep this copy of the painting?"

"Sure," Claire replied.

"Thanks for telling me your story." Sophie gave Claire a hug, then stood up and walked out of the theater with her long hair tumbling down her back.

Claire remained in her seat, staring at the empty stage. The dancing girls created by her imagination had departed. Sophie's eyes were full of fire when she said she wouldn't testify unless the person responsible for June's death was incarcerated. There was plenty of guilt to go around, but how could anyone other than the drug dealer be held legally responsible for June's death? What made Sophie think anyone would ever be locked up?

Claire stared at the stage, trying to apply cool logic to the death of June Reid. There had been no signs of physical violence. If there was a murder, it hadn't required force or strength. But someone could have deliberately locked Maia in the room with the China White, knowing that left alone there she would become claustrophobic, panic, shoot up, and OD. All that would have been necessary to carry out this diabolical plan was cold calculation and hard cash. The murderer could have been anyone heartless or angry enough to pull it off, a man or a woman. That person might have used the rationalization that Maia was a homeless person and an addict, which made her dispensable. The person who had admitted to turning the deadbolt was Paul Begala, but he claimed he didn't know Maia was in the room. He could have been lying and he could also have had a motive for wanting Maia dead. If Paul had been having sex with her it would have cost him his job and devastated his sick wife. On the other hand someone from June's past or present could have paid him or intimidated him into locking the door. The person who seemed to know the most about the details of Maia's life was Ansia. If only Claire could find her.

She had the sensation that the curtain had come down; the stage had gone dark but the lights had come on in the rest of the theater.

# Chapter Twenty-five

That evening Claire worked late, then went to Century 14 Downtown to see a movie with a friend. Afterward they had dinner at Tucanos, where the waiters went from table to table slicing grilled meat and fish off skewers and onto plates. The food was delicious. The smiling waiters and flashing knives were theater. As always there was a long wait to get in. By the time dinner was over, it was nearly ten o'clock.

As she drove across Central, Claire's thoughts returned to Ansia, who might have been one of the last people to talk to Maia. Where did a homeless woman who could not — or would not — go to a shelter sleep? Would there be times when she would have the money or could get a john to pay for a motel room? It was warm enough in the summer to sleep outside. Would she find more safety in a secluded spot on campus or a crowded spot near Central? How hard did campus security look for people sleeping in all the wrong places? Would anyone notice or care if she slept somewhere near Central? Bill Hartley had said he found her there in the backseat of a car. Did she always go to the same car in the same place? Claire tried to imagine where she herself would sleep if she were homeless, but her imagination failed her. Bill Hartley had made more progress in one visit to Albuquerque than Claire, who worked within walking distance from Central, had in weeks. It was time for her to do more than hand out photocopies and business cards and wait for Ansia to come to her.

When she got to the university Claire parked on Central near the only restaurant that was still open, the Frontier. Light shining from the windows gave it the lonely glow of an Edward Hopper painting. The Frontier was the first place in the morning to find a cup of coffee and the last place at night to find a touch of warmth. Given its location it had to deal with the homeless. Like the library it tended to ignore them unless they caused trouble.

Claire went inside and found the Frontier was almost empty. A young woman with a heart tattooed on her upper arm stood at the cash register. Her T-shirt was cropped short enough to show the ring through her navel. Claire asked her if Ansia ever came to the Frontier.

"Who?" the clerk asked while her fingers danced across the counter.

"Ansia. She's a homeless woman whose hair is streaked the color of cherry Jell-O," Claire said.

"Why do you want to know?" The fingers stopped their restless motion.

"I want to help her."

The young woman gave a stare Claire found incomprehensible. Then she turned her hands over on the counter palms up. It took a while for Claire, who had never paid for information before, to figure out what the woman wanted. When she rubbed her thumb and middle finger together in the universal gesture of greed, Claire got the message, took a twenty from her purse and placed it in the clerk's palm. The woman rubbed her fingers together again and Claire forked over another twenty.

The fingers closed into a fist, the money crunched, and the woman said, "She sleeps in a junk car parked beside the Dumpster in the alley parking lot. Back there." She pointed behind the building. "The owner rents her the backseat for ten bucks a month. It makes her feel like she has a home."

"Have you seen her recently?" Claire asked.

"No, it's been a while."

Claire thanked the woman and left the restaurant. Thinking she might need more cash, she went to the ATM machine and took the maximum withdrawal her bank would allow in twenties, the price of a BB of heroin or a nugget of information.

She returned to her truck and drove around the corner to the Frontier's parking lot where a sign read RESERVED FOR PATRONS ONLY. The back wall of the Frontier was painted with a flowered mural that included clumps of pink and red hollyhocks. They seemed to be the quintessential New Mexican flower, but Claire knew that hollyhocks were actually transplants from North Africa. She supposed that if a woman were very drugged she might imagine herself to be in a garden back here. During the day it was nearly impossible to find a parking space in this lot, but tonight there were only four cars.

Claire turned the corner into an alley where she found a darker, emptier lot. A Dumpster in the far corner was shadowed by nearby trees. A gray wreck of a Chrysler hunkered down beside it. Claire parked, took her flashlight from the glove compartment, closed the door to her truck as quietly as possible, walked to the Chrysler, and peered through the rear window. There was enough light from the streetlamps in the alley to see the shape of a body under a blanket, asleep, dead, or drugged out. Although the windows and doors were closed, the car exuded a pungent smell. Claire hoped it wasn't the smell of death. How long would a woman have to be dead in this car before anyone noticed? The smell could always be blamed on the nearby Dumpster.

She took a deep breath and tapped the

window. There was no verbal response, no movement in the backseat. Claire tugged at the door handle and found the door locked. She beamed her flashlight through the window onto the blanket. The person beneath it squirmed and turned away from the light but Claire held it steady until Ansia sat up and blinked her eyes. Her pupils were dilated by drugs or the flashlight.

Thank God, Claire thought, she's still alive. She turned the flashlight toward her own face to demonstrate that she was not a threat.

"I work in the library," Claire mouthed through the glass. "I need to talk to you."

"What about?" Ansia's voice was slurred.

"Maia."

"She's dead."

"I know. I need to know how she died, and who talked to you about her. Can you open the window or door so we can talk? I'll give you some money, take you to a motel for the night. You can take a shower if you want to. I'll wash your clothes."

Ansia stared at Claire, then reached over and rolled down the window, releasing more of the nose-burning odor, which Claire now identified as the ammonia smell of urine. Ansia peed on herself to keep the men away.

"You and Maia were friends, weren't you?" Claire asked.

Ansia nodded yes. Claire turned the flashlight down so it wasn't shining in her face. Plastic bags full of belongings littered the floor.

"Did someone talk to you about her before she died?" Claire asked.

Ansia nodded again. "A man came here."

"What did he want?"

"He wanted to know how to find her. He said her name was June, but the woman he described to me was Maia. I wouldn't tell him where she slept. I wouldn't send a man there. I told him to look for her in the downtown library in the daytime."

"What did the man look like?" Claire asked.

"He had brown hair. He was a runner."

So far it confirmed Bill Hartley's story. "How did Maia get into the library at night? Do you know?" Claire asked.

"The man with the white in his hair gave her his numbers."

"Seth Malcolm?"

"I don't remember his name."

"How often did Maia sleep there?"

"All the time. I wouldn't go there myself."

"Why not?"

Ansia grinned and Claire could see the holes where her teeth had once been. "Too many men in the library. Men are dogs. They think they are God's dogs, but they are just dogs."

"There are men around here, too, aren't there?" Claire asked.

"They don't bother me here. I smell, but when I smell too bad in the library they throw me out. I lock my door here." Ansia sat up straight and dropped her blanket. "This is my home. I pay rent. I don't need to go to a motel. Just give me the money."

"I'll do both if you want," Claire said.

Ansia shook her head. "I only want the money."

Claire handed her a hundred dollars in twenties, the price of almost a year of rent or of several days' worth of drugs. She wished she didn't know exactly how much a twenty would buy on the street. "Can I take you to a restaurant? Buy you something to eat?" she asked.

"I'll buy myself some dog food. If you want to know more, you'll have to give me more money."

"There's more?"

Ansia nodded.

Claire handed over five more twenties.

"A woman came here, too," Ansia said. "Later. After the man. She also said she was looking for June, but I knew she meant Maia. She was looking for her little girl. She wanted to find out where her little lost baby daughter lived, she said. I told her about the paintings on Central. If she could find her daughter in a painting there and show me which one it was, I said I would help her."

"Did you tell Maia the woman was looking for her?"

"No. It was after hours, and I don't like to go into the library then. If the guards see me, they throw me out."

Besides, Claire thought, she had valuable information to trade for money and money meant drugs.

"The woman came back to me with the painting. She saw my painting in the gallery, too, and told me how pretty I looked." As Ansia preened and smoothed her cherry Jell-O hair, Claire witnessed the indestructible nature of vanity. When there was nothing else left but smoke and ash, there would still be vanity. "She showed me her daughter dancing in a circle. I knew that was Maia. I told the mother where she could find her little girl. I told her about the man in the library who could let her in." Ansia's proud grin said that on the street that had made her a hero.

"Did she give you anything in exchange for that information?" Claire asked.

"She gave me *medicina*."

"Medicine?"

Ansia nodded. When her body was too unappealing to sell, that left her only information to trade. Claire had given her money, the woman had given her drugs, but when you got right down to it what was the difference?

"Was it China White?" Claire asked.

"It was very white." Ansia grinned.

"It killed Maia, but it didn't kill you," Claire said. "Why?"

"Maia kicked. The white was too strong for her, but me, I'm still all tore up from the floor up."

"Can you tell me what the woman looked like?"

"She wore a hat. Her hair was darker, but she coulda been Maia's mother. She coulda." Ansia's tone became defensive, then turned hopelessly sad. "But a mother wouldn't give her daughter China White. That woman was a murderer, not a mother." For an instant Ansia's expression was a silent scream that registered the total despair of her life and Maia's death. Then she found the solution and began to collect her plastic bags. "I have to go," she said.

"Where?" Claire asked. "Can I give you a ride?"

"No. I have to go right now."

Ansia pushed open the door and climbed out of the Chrysler with the bags in her hands. Claire, who didn't know how to stop her, heard the bags rustling as Ansia scurried down the alley. The smell of a fouled nest lingered until Claire closed the door. She'd learned what she needed to learn and done what she had to do, but she hated the way she'd had to do it.

* * *

She was glad she had a bed to curl up in when she got home, but the dreams she had took her far away from percale sheets and the warmth of her cat. They took her back to the street, to plastic bags, dirt, fine white powder, and the tracks a needle makes in an addict's eyeballs and arms.

Claire woke up as the sun came over the mountain, glad to leave those dreams behind. She got up and made herself a cup of coffee, thinking about what she could do to help. Ansia needed clothing and food. Claire went to her closet first and began looking for clothes that would fit Ansia, who was smaller than she was and thin as a street dog. Claire had no idea what kind of clothes Ansia might like, but style shouldn't be the issue, anyway; comfort and endurability were more important. At first Claire looked for clothes she could no longer fit into. There weren't many — a few that had shrunk, hardly any that had been outgrown. In recent years Claire had gained little weight.

Next she searched for clothes that had gone out of style, but she didn't find many of those, either. Her style had remained simple and classic. As she pulled hangers along the rack, the search took her into the back of the closet where clothes with bad memories attached to them like markdown tags ended up. She yanked out the black dress she'd worn to the funeral of her ex-husband's mother. She hated that dress and never wanted to wear it again. Her hand was on the collar when she realized there were likely to be more deaths in Evan's family. Why buy a new dress to hate when she already had this one? Besides, Ansia's life was morbid enough without dressing in black. Ansia should wear colors.

Claire's hand went to a pink silk shirt she had last worn during a humiliating encounter with her boss, Harrison Hough. The price on that garment got slashed and slashed again every time Harrison embarrassed her. The person pink would have looked best on was Maia, not Ansia, and Claire was too practical to give anyone silk to wear on the street. She reached deeper into the bad-memory corner of the closet. Many of the clothes there were connected with men, but there was also a melon colored T-shirt worn on the day an old friend from college had ripped her off. That T-shirt would work for Ansia; it wouldn't fight with the cherry Jell-O hair. But how could she give a T-shirt full of bad vibes to a woman whose life was already desperate?

Claire's hand returned to the front of the closet where she kept the clothes that she liked and wore. She had so much and Ansia had so little. It didn't mean anything to give away the clothes she hated. There was no sacrifice or atonement in discarding marked-down rejects. She skipped her jeans — too hard to fit — and picked out two loose cotton dresses she liked, a few T-shirts, and some cotton drawstring pants. The colors of sage and beige would compliment Ansia's hair. She knew she was acting like a mother dressing a daughter with a future to go off to school. It was an illusion; anything Ansia wore would turn to dirt and rags on the street. But it was a gesture Claire needed to make.

Wondering where to put the clothes, she went to the cupboard where she stored her plastic bags. The bags from Smith's were too fragile. The bags from Whole Foods were stronger but represented too much affluence, not the right message for a person to be carrying around the street. Why did it have to be a plastic shopping bag anyway? In the hall closet Claire found a more durable black vinyl shoulder bag she had gotten at a conference and put the clothes inside.

Then she went to the kitchen looking for food that was nourishing and wouldn't spoil, picking out a bag of granola, a bag of nuts, a jar of peanut butter, a box of whole wheat crackers. She added some health food bars, carrot sticks, and a ripe mango. The mango would spoil, but Claire put it in because it was delicious. She added a dull paring knife for peeling the mango. She put the food in a Smith's bag and added it to the shoulder bag.

Before she went to work, she drove down Central, pulled into the lot on the alley behind the Frontier restaurant, and parked beside the Chrysler. It was early enough that the lot was still empty. The door to the car was unlocked. Claire assumed Ansia didn't have a key and only locked the doors when she was inside. The owner of the car wouldn't want her to be able to drive it. It was a kind gesture for that person to let her sleep in the car, far more comfortable and secure than sleeping on the street. Ansia's blanket was on the seat and it bore the impression of a curled-up body. It was a fetal shape, the shape of a conch shell, a shape that represented the search for security.

Claire placed her bag on the backseat, leaving her card on top, aware that she was acting like a foolish mother who thought if she could dress and nourish she could save. But Maia was already abused and dead and the odds of saving Ansia were terrible. Someone out there was pretending to be a mother, a dark mother reaching out like the shadow in the painting and giving away a deadly white powder. In myth a man chased the girls into the sky. In reality Maia had been pursued by a woman. Had she intended to kill Ansia, too? Would she come back when she found out she had not? Was finding this woman the only way to protect Ansia? This could be the person who had to be incarcerated before Sophie Roybal could safely tell her story.

# Chapter Twenty-six

Claire left the lot and drove to her own parking space behind the library. Her first stop when she got inside was Celia's office. She knew exactly how Celia would react to Ansia's story that the man with the white in his hair was the one who gave Maia the code. The outburst would be better expressed outside the halls of CSWR. Celia wore a print dress today with blue shoes that reminded Claire of Dorothy dancing off to see the Wizard of Oz. She was busy working on her computer and didn't notice Claire until she cleared her throat.

"We need to talk," Claire said.

"What about?" Celia asked.

"Seth Malcolm. Let's go outside."

"It's that bad?"

"Yes."

Claire led Celia out of the library's main entrance. There was no place Celia could explode on campus without attracting attention, but at least outside the attention wouldn't be from Harrison Hough. Claire was headed for a bench beside the duck pond, but as soon as they were out the door, Celia stopped her.

"Tell me now and get it over with," she said.

"I found Ansia sleeping in a parked car behind the Frontier last night and we talked. She described a man who looks like Seth as the one who gave Maia the code."

"Goddamn him," Celia said. The students walking by were too engrossed in their cell phones to pay much attention to her outburst. "What in the hell was he thinking?"

"I'd say thinking is the wrong word for it," Claire replied. "Ansia told me a woman claiming to be Maia's mother came looking for her. She told the woman about Seth and told her how to find Maia. In return the woman gave Ansia China White."

"You think that's how Maia got it?"

"Yes, and I think that if she found herself locked in a room with China White she would have taken it. Locking her in may have been a deliberate act, not the accident Paul Begala claims. Ansia said Maia slept in the library all the time. She wouldn't have let Paul lock her in more than once."

"Seth has been working in the stacks recently. Let's see if we can find him."

They went back inside. Celia marched to the elevator and punched in her code, and they took the elevator down to the stacks, where scholars burrowed among the books. Celia's blue shoes wove a path through the section of leather-bound ledgers with gold embossing on the spines. When there was no other paper available on reservations in the nineteenth century, Plains Indians painted their ponies and their lives on ledger paper with the numbers and records as background. Claire loved ledger art and would have preferred to think about these books than the confrontation looming with Seth. It was too reminiscent of the day she confronted her husband about his lies and his affair. She knew what followed accusations — denial, denial, and more denial — and then the blame was turned on the accuser. When the husband is guilty, the wife gets the blame.

They left the ledger section and entered the shelves where documents were stored in plain brown boxes, went around a corner, and came upon an office Seth had created by pushing boxes aside and clearing a place on a shelf. He wasn't at his bookshelf desk, but he'd left behind a stack of papers with notes about Tobiah James.

Celia picked up the papers and snapped them for emphasis. "It's a privilege and an honor for Seth to have access to this information and this room. He has done nothing but abuse it."

"What do we do now?" Claire asked.

"Wait and see if he comes back. He may have gone to the men's room." Celia looked through the papers, tapping her toe against the floor while she waited.

Claire stared at the rows of brown boxes until Seth came around the corner wearing khaki pants and a white short-sleeved T-shirt.

When he saw Celia holding his papers, he burst out, "What are you doing? That's my dissertation."

"It *was* your dissertation," Celia replied. "Your right to use the stacks is about to be revoked. And you could lose your fellowship, too."

"What'd I do?" The color drained out of Seth's face, leaving him looking as pale as his T-shirt.

"'What did I do?' " Celia mimicked his anxious tone. "You gave a homeless woman your code. She went into the basement and she died there."

"I don't know what you're talking about." Seth raised his chin in denial.

"Ansia told me about your relationship with Maia," Claire said.

"Ansia's an addict," Seth replied. "You can't believe anything she says."

"Oh, but I can," Celia said. "I'm the one who gives out the codes. When it comes to granting access to the stacks, I'm the judge and I'm the jury."

Claire knew that wasn't quite true. Celia was prone to exaggeration in her clothes and her statements. She didn't have the right to arbitrarily take away anyone's code. Seth could appeal and, like everything else at the library, the issue would be decided by committee. But he knew that even the accusation would be damaging. Another committee would decide whether or not to grant him a Ph.D., and members of the two committees were certain to be acquainted.

"I felt sorry for Maia," he admitted. "She was an intelligent person. I helped her out. Is that so terrible? What harm did she ever do to anybody?"

"She cut a valuable illustration out of a rare book," Claire reminded him.

"I'm sorry about that. Really. I'll pay the library back for it, if that's what you want."

"How?" Celia asked. "By selling drugs?"

"I don't sell drugs."

Claire noticed that his bare arms were free of scabs, scars, and needle marks. Seth rubbed his hand across the top of his head and his premature white spot seemed to spread. Claire had the impression that if they kept him here long enough all the hair on his head would turn white.

"Maia was interested in Tobiah James. She would have been a great student, but she couldn't get into UNM," Seth said. "I fell behind on my research and she helped me. I let her into the Anderson Reading Room and then when she needed a place to sleep I gave her my code."

"How long had that been going on?" Celia asked.

"Couple of months, I guess."

"Where was she sleeping all that time?" Claire asked. "She couldn't have been letting Paul Begala lock her into the storage room every night."

"I don't know where she slept," Seth said. "It could have been anywhere in the basement. It might have been safer to move from place to place. Maybe that's what she did."

"Did you ever tell anyone that Maia was sleeping in the basement?" Claire asked.

Seth's eyes went from Celia to Claire as if trying to estimate what other damaging information they had. Celia crossed her arms and tapped her fingers against the sleeve of her dress. Her fierce glare said the only way out for him was to tell the whole truth.

He fessed up. "One day when I left the Anderson Reading Room, I found a woman waiting outside. She told me she was Maia's mother and asked if I could help her find her daughter. They were estranged, she said, but there had been a family crisis and she had to find Maia. She knew her daughter needed help and she was hoping for a reconciliation."

"What did she offer you in exchange for that information?" Celia asked.

"Nothing. She offered me nothing and she gave me nothing. She told me she was Maia's mother, and I believed her. I was just trying to help."

Celia's expression remained dubious but Claire was inclined to believe him. She saw Seth as a person all too likely to bend to the will of others. Too much accommodating to too many others could explain why he was in so much trouble and why his dissertation remained unfinished.

"What did the woman look like?" Claire asked.

"She looked as if she could be Maia's mother. She was old enough." He stared at his inquisitors as if he was thinking "as old as you are," but he didn't say so. "She had blondish hair. She was about your height," he said to Claire. "Like Maia, she was a quiet-looking, inconspicuous person. She didn't wear any makeup. You wouldn't notice her except that she had on large glasses with square black frames. The one thing I really remember about her is those ugly glasses. She would have been an attractive woman without those glasses."

"Did you notice the color of her eyes?" Claire asked.

"No."

"What was she wearing?"

"Jeans and a shirt, I guess."

The woman Ansia described had darker hair and Ansia hadn't mentioned the glasses. The woman could have been wearing a disguise on one or both occasions or there could have been more than one woman. Ansia might not be considered a reliable witness, but she hadn't been wrong about Bill Hartley. "Did the woman offer you any proof that she was Maia's mother?" Claire asked.

"She showed me a painting of a group of girls dancing in a circle. I recognized one of them as a younger Maia."

Claire felt weak when she heard that, like her emotions were draining into a pool on the floor. Ansia had provided the information about Seth and the painting. Lisa Teague's beautiful portrait had been used to find and kill the woman who posed for it. In exchange for what? The chance to be a hero on the street? A BB of China White? For an addict there was no justice, no friendship, no loyalty. For an addict the only truth was *la jeringa y la chiva*.

"I believed her," Seth said. "She came back that night. I didn't give her the code. I only let her in once. I don't know what happened after that. I don't even know if she and Maia connected. Maia died of a drug overdose, right? Nobody made her take it. Nobody twisted her arm. Nobody beat her up. Okay, I shouldn't have let her or the woman in, but what did that have to do with Maia's death?"

Everything, Claire thought, but she didn't say so. There was still a police investigation going on and she was afraid she and Celia had already strayed too far into Detective Owen's territory.

"Shouldn't you be talking to Paul Begala?" Seth asked. "He's the one who locked the door, not me."

"I'll be talking to him, too," Celia said.

"What about my code?" Seth pleaded. "Can I keep it?"

"I haven't made that decision yet." Celia turned to Claire. "Let's go," she said.

Before they rounded the corner into the next aisle, Claire looked back and saw Seth sitting in his chair slumped over his make-shift desk, clutching his head in his hands.

# Chapter Twenty-seven

Claire followed Celia to the door that led deeper into the basement. Celia punched in her code and blinking green lights indicated they had gained admittance. Looking over Celia's shoulder Claire could easily read her numbers. The woman claiming to be Maia's mother could have done the same thing with Seth. To let her in once was to let her in for as long as his code was in effect. They were in the maintenance sector now near the furnace where pipes marked CHILLED WATER RETURN snaked under the ceiling. This was where the ghost of the woman in the pinafore dress — the first librarian — was known to wander. Someone had drawn a scowling face on the wall and labeled it THE PLUMBER. Red lights flashed EXIT over the doorways and roaches lay belly-up on the floor. This was the part of the basement where maintenance had to work, but most people avoided it.

"Goddamn that boy," Celia said.

"What are you going to do about it?" Claire asked.

"Report him to Harrison. I have to. I'm not about to lose my job over Seth Malcolm.

You know that Harrison doesn't take insubordination lightly. Seth will be locked out of the stacks and he'll lose his fellowship." She stopped and faced Claire. "Who do you think this woman is going around handing out drugs, looking for Maia? Could it really be her mother?"

"Not unless the body found in the Rio Grande Gorge wasn't Veronica Reid. I heard it was badly mangled. But you'd think the police would have definitely identified the victim. Given the timing of Maia's death — right before June was scheduled to talk to the Taos DA — I'd say it was someone who didn't want her to testify against Damon Fitzgerald."

"How did anybody know she was going to testify?"

"Bill Hartley talked her into meeting with the DA. He knew. His wife knew. Word might have leaked from the DA's office. In a small town like Taos everybody seems to know exactly what everybody else is doing. The woman could have been one or more of the mothers in Taos who didn't want the scandal to break and expose their own daughters. She could have been someone trying to protect Damon Fitzgerald or Edward Girard or even Paul Begala. I think the glasses were a diversion. Except for that detail the descriptions were generic. Average height, average looks, middle age. Some people think all middle-aged women look alike."

"Let's see if Paul can tell us more."

"Is that where we're going now? To talk to Paul?"

"Yes."

Claire hesitated. "Don't you think we ought to talk to Detective Owen first? There is an investigation going on."

"Not that I've noticed," Celia snapped. "The codes and the locks are my responsibility. Overseeing the security system is my job. I'm the one Harrison blames for Maia's presence in the basement. By the time Detective Owen gets here, Seth could talk to Paul and give him all the excuse he needs to shut up. I need to get to him first. Are you with me?"

Claire didn't share Celia's conviction, but she couldn't let her go to Paul's office alone, either. She followed the blue shoes down the long, dingy basement corridors, imagining how debilitating it would be to spend all day working here. Claire rarely entered the maintenance sector. She found the narrow halls with the pipes throbbing overhead oppressive, although it was possible that to a person seeking comfort the throbbing pipes might resemble a beating heart. She felt the weight of the library resting on her shoulders down here, but Celia seemed energized by the chase. Seth had said that Maia had been sleeping in the basement for months. As Claire walked, she looked for another place as secluded as the storage room where Maia had died, but she didn't find one.

When they got to Paul's office they found him sitting in a swivel chair at his desk. He spun around as he heard them approach. Once again Claire had the sensation that only one of his eyes focused, but he saw enough to turn his expression guarded. Paul's shoulders tightened in the gesture of a besieged animal hunkering down, waiting, watching. He had tacked magazine photos of outdoor scenes on his office walls — a rippling trout stream, views from mountain peaks, a vast green forest. One of the photos was of Paul himself casting a fishing line out over a stream. Claire saw the photos as windows out of the dreary basement.

"Did you see a woman in the basement looking for Maia shortly before she died?" Celia jumped right in without even pausing to say hello.

Claire visualized her words wrapped inside a bubble hanging over the office. She sympathized with Celia's impatience and her anger, but her intuition told her those were the wrong words.

They gave Paul the opportunity to answer "I see women down here all the time. Librarians, students, professors. I don't make a note of everybody I see. My job is maintenance, not surveillance. Nobody ever told me she was looking for Maia."

Celia was too committed to her pursuit to slow down now. "This woman claimed to be Maia's mother."

"How'd she get in?"

"Someone let her in."

"Well, I can tell you this much. It wasn't me."

Now Claire had the uneasy sensation that one of his eyes had focused on Celia and the other on her. She'd been hovering in the doorway hoping Paul wouldn't notice her presence. She wanted to be like a bird in one of his photographs, who could watch without being observed herself.

"We only have your word that you didn't know Maia was in the storage room," Celia said. "Suppose the woman wanted Maia to stay locked up in there and persuaded someone to turn the deadbolt?"

Claire wished she had a way to counter Celia's bad-cop act. The only thing that came to mind was to ask Paul about the outdoor photos, but she knew Celia would consider that an intrusion and an unwelcome diversion. Claire kept quiet, observing Paul's body language.

He remained watchful and wary, but he wasn't crumpling the way Seth had. Celia didn't have the power over maintenance that she had over graduate students. Paul Begala didn't have to answer to her and he knew it.

"I locked the door to the storage room on Friday like I always do when I leave here," he insisted. "I went fishing over the weekend. Even if I had come in, I had no reason to check that room. I opened the door on Tuesday when I got back. I found the body. I notified the police. I didn't talk to any woman claiming to be Maia's mother or any-body else's mother. And I never saw Maia in the storage room or anywhere else in the basement."

Celia moved on, appearing to change the subject. "How's your wife doing?" she asked. "Does she like the home she's in now?"

"Better than the other one. What's that got to do with anything?" Paul asked.

"Just curious," Celia said.

Paul's cell phone rang. He picked it up, listened briefly, then replied, "I'll be right there." He turned toward to Celia. "Anything else? There's an emergency near the tower, a leak that has to be fixed right now."

"Could someone have taken your key and used it or made a copy?" Celia asked.

"Like who? The librarian in the pinafore who haunts this place? Maybe she's the mother you've been looking for. These keys here? While I'm at work they never leave my side." Paul shook the ring with jangly sound. "Now, if you don't mind, ladies, I have a job to do."

They left the office. Paul locked the door behind them with an ostentatious rattle of the key chain, then walked down the corridor whistling an unidentifiable tune. Claire saw a door nearby with a red EXIT sign over it and a ramp that led outside.

"Let's go out here," she said to Celia. "I can't face walking back through the tunnels again." She had an overpowering longing to see sky over her head instead of pipes marked CHILLED WATER RETURN.

"All right."

Once they were outside in the fresh air behind the library, Celia said, "My gut reaction is that Paul was lying. What do you think?"

Claire had gotten a different perspective from her bird's-eye perch. "I'm not sure he was telling the whole truth," she said. "But I wouldn't necessarily say he was lying."

"I think the APD needs to check his bank accounts and see if any money was deposited around the time that Maia died."

"If there was any money, most likely it was paid in cash and spent as cash," Claire said, remembering how the painting was purchased. "Nursing care is unbelievably expensive. Do you think Paul could possibly have been paid enough to change the kind of care his wife gets?"

"When you're desperate anything helps," Celia said.

"True," Claire said. "I agree that we should contact Detective Owen. Do you want to do it or should I?"

"I'll do it," Celia said. "Monitoring the codes is my responsibility."

# Chapter Twenty-eight

Claire was busy with meetings and phone calls until the end of the day, when she found herself sitting at her desk, staring at her computer screen. The books-with-wings screen saver had clicked off and the screen was blank. All it took to pull images from the darkness was a click of the keys. If Claire clicked the right keys, she might even find images that would help in the investigation. Ansia could evaluate the images — if Claire could find her again.

She left the library and walked across campus, passing the Student Union, then the bookstore. She crossed the dividing line of Central and entered the parking lot behind the Frontier restaurant. The painted hollyhocks were still in bloom. The parking places were all taken. Claire walked to the alley parking lot and found the Chrysler in place.

Trying to care for Ansia reminded her of caring for a stray cat. You put out food at night and checked to see if it was gone in the morning. Sometimes the caregiver went for days without seeing the cat. The only way to know it was still alive was if the food had been eaten. Claire peered through the dirty window of the Chrysler. The blanket was in the backseat. The black bag and her card were gone. Ansia could have come back or someone else might have taken them.

As she turned away from the car, Claire caught a glimpse of a black strap hanging over the edge of the Dumpster. Part of her wanted to walk away and not know any more, but she made herself go to the Dumpster and peer over the edge into the pile of stinking garbage. Death stank, but Claire didn't know how to identify that smell. She had a stomach-churning anxiety that she might find cherry Jell-O hair and rotting flesh among the garbage, but all she saw was the basic pile of trash and an empty black bag. Was that a sign that Ansia had rejected her gift? Knowing better than to apply the rules of society to people who lived on the street, Claire dismissed the thought. If you're going to give, she told herself, you do it for the sake of giving, not for the sake of getting a return. She wasn't looking for gratitude. She was looking for information. The clothes and food she'd left in the bag were gone. Claire hoped it was Ansia who had taken them. She wouldn't want to come across someone else wearing her clothes on the street.

Deciding it was useless to leave another card, she reached into her purse and pulled out a notepad and a pen. "Ansia," she wrote. "You can help me identify the woman who was looking for Maia. I'll be working late. Please come to the library and ask for me at the Information Desk. It's important. Thank you. Claire Reynier."

She left the note in the backseat, crossed the parking lot, and walked back to the library. As she passed the Jimenez statue of the woman dancing in a swirling skirt, Claire asked herself why she felt such a strong sense of anxiety about Ansia. She hoped it wouldn't turn out to be a premonition. Ansia lived a dangerous life on the street, but she had survival skills. She had a home of sorts with a door she could lock. She'd survived the deadly China White, but suppose the person who gave it to her came back with something even finer and even more dangerous? Was there anything finer? Detective Owen had said China White was a West Coast drug rarely seen in Albuquerque. It came from someplace more populated, Claire thought, someplace more cosmopolitan and more affluent, someplace where addicts could afford a better class of drugs.

She hoped Celia had called Detective Owen. Claire felt that they were in over their heads now and that Ansia needed more than clothes and food. She needed protection. Celia had tried with Seth and Paul, but Owen was a more skillful interrogator. Claire felt Celia had given up too much when she asked Paul Begala if he'd seen a woman claiming to be Maia's mother in the basement because now he knew exactly what he needed to deny. It would have been better to ask if he had seen anyone suspicious without revealing just who she was looking for. It was Celia's nature to jump right in, but Owen waited and watched, letting the suspect set her own trap. Claire suspected the detective knew exactly why she herself had taken such a strong interest in the story of Maia. But Celia, who was a good friend, had no idea. Owen dealt with violence and abuse on a daily basis. Celia did not.

Claire stopped at the Information Desk and asked the student working there to call her if Ansia showed up. Like everyone else who worked at the library, the student knew of Ansia.

"Are you sure you want to talk to *her?*" he asked.

"Yes," Claire replied.

When she reached her office, she shut the door behind her, called Celia, and asked if she had spoken to Detective Owen.

"Not yet, but I left a message," she replied.

Claire hung up and turned toward her computer, tapping the keys to see what images she could pull from the darkness, hoping a Google search would determine whether any of the people connected to Maia went to the West Coast before Memorial Day. She was looking for information to give

Detective Owen when she called back and for pictures to show Ansia. Claire had read somewhere that the main Google office had a screen displaying all the words being searched at any given moment, providing an overview of the world's ever shifting interest. The most popular searches were of well-known celebrities, although occasionally the name of a lesser-known celebrity showed up as the answer to a question on a quiz show.

The names she was searching would have very low priority on the Google scale. The most famous person connected to Maia and the one person Claire knew would appear on a search engine was Edward Girard, who had told her he was setting up an installation at MOCA, the Museum of Contemporary Art, in Los Angeles. If a person were in the market for top-of-the-line designer heroin, L.A. would be as good a place as any to look. Given the name, the China White probably came from Asia, making it even more likely to be sold on the West Coast. Although Edward hadn't been a model of familial devotion, Claire found it hard to believe that he could be responsible for giving heroin to his own daughter. Nevertheless she entered his name in the search engine.

There were many entries for Edward Girard, making it difficult to tell if any had been added since her last search. She came across the Web site for MOCA, which announced that Edward Girard's installation would open in September. The museum's Web site did not reveal if or when Edward had been in town to help with the installation.

Claire moved on to Jennifer Rule, who might well have accompanied Edward on his trips to the West Coast. She'd come to Albuquerque with him. She had the schizophrenic job of promoting the artist at the same time that she needed to shelter him. Did she want to protect him badly enough to try to prevent the scandal that would follow June's testimony about Damon Fitzgerald? June died right before the Maximum Moon celebration and a few months in advance of Edward's museum exhibition. It was a time of maximum achievement for Edward. It wouldn't reflect well on him to have it known that he'd ignored his daughter and she'd been abused by her mother's boyfriend in Taos. But Claire had no idea if Jennifer even knew he had a daughter.

If Edward had been telling the truth, he didn't know what had become of June in Taos, but it hadn't taken Claire long to find out. She had been struck by Jennifer's odd reaction to the photocopy of *Summertime*, the way she treated it as if was an annoying and threatening bug. It could have been because Edward admired the artist and Jennifer saw talented women as competition. Or had she seen the painting as a threat to Edward's career and her job? Claire didn't consider

Jennifer a middle-aged woman, but she wasn't looking at her from the perspective of a graduate student. She didn't see Jennifer as a plain, nearly invisible person, either, but she could visualize her wearing large black glasses and a hat. She could also imagine the ambitious and focused Jennifer considering a homeless person a nonperson.

Claire entered the name Jennifer Rule and learned that she was as good about getting her own name out there as she was about publicizing Edward Girard's. Whenever Edward's name was mentioned, Jennifer's was likely to be connected to it. She had her own slick and professional Web site, which included a photograph showing every chestnut-colored hair in place. Claire made a note of Jennifer's URL, then printed out the photo.

From Jennifer's Web site Claire learned that she was the publicist for several artists. Edward Girard was the biggest name on Jennifer's client list, which didn't necessarily mean he was the biggest moneymaker. The museum installation would be prestigious but Edward was unlikely to make much money on it. Although Spiral Rocks was magnificent, Edward didn't charge admission. Jennifer promoted Edward's installations, as well as a book about his work, on her Web site. And there was something else Claire learned from Jennifer's Web site that she had yet to see in the articles about Edward. Filming would begin soon at

Spiral Rocks for a PBS documentary.

Claire printed out that page, too. Next she searched the name Bettina Hartley. She hadn't considered Bettina middle-aged either, but that was an image makeup — or lack of makeup — could change. The only place she found the name Bettina Hartley was on Web sites devoted to class reunions and genealogy. Claire tried Bettina's husband, Bill, and learned what she already knew: He was a ski instructor in Taos who had won an Iron Man Triathlon. The Triathlon had its own Web site and on it Claire found a picture of Bill accepting his trophy. Bettina stood behind him with her blond hair tied back in a ponytail. She looked even younger in this photograph than she did in person. Claire printed it out anyway; if nothing else a positive ID of Bill would be useful.

Next she searched the all too common names of Maureen and Nancy Prescott, but nothing of value came up. She tried the even more common name of Sharon Miller, getting fifty thousand hits, which was about as useful as getting none. Claire was curious about where Sharon lived before she moved into her getaway house in Taos with Damon Fitzgerald. She called Sophie Roybal to ask.

Sophie happened to be at home and her voice was far more welcoming this time. "I'm glad we had the chance to meet and talk," she said.

"Me, too," Claire replied. "I hope we can do it again. Could you tell me where Sharon Miller lived before she moved to Taos?"

"It was in the Bay Area near San Francisco, but I don't know exactly where."

"What was the creative career she pursued without success?"

"She tried to be an actress. When she first came to Taos she appeared in some amateur productions, but then she gave that up and decided to make Damon her career."

"Thanks," Claire said. "Please call next time you come to Albuquerque."

"I plan to," Sophie promised.

Claire had learned what she needed to know about Sharon Miller, but not everything she needed to know about Damon Fitzgerald. His name was her next search. She was sure Jennifer would be gratified to learn that Edward Girard had produced far more hits. Damon appeared mostly as a speaker at alternative housing conferences, but Claire also found his name on a Web site for the Center of Light Chapel, not in the prominent position of the Phoenix architect who won the commission, but in a discussion of the designs that were rejected. The committee wanted a dome that reached for the sky and Damon's design was considered cavelike and uninspiring. One critic went so far as to label it dull. The criticism raised the question in Claire's mind of whether it was a humiliating public rejection that started Damon on his spiral of abuse. Or was it the confirmation of something he might have already suspected — that he didn't have the talent to be an important architect?

Claire printed out that page and continued her search. On the more recent site of a conference about the use of solar energy she found Damon listed as keynote speaker. Speaking was something at which he excelled. There was a photo of him smiling for the camera. The conference took place from May 16 to May 20 in San Francisco. Claire checked the list of attendees and was not at all surprised to find Sharon Miller's name there. She hoped to find a picture of her on the site, too. Sharon was not on the presenters' page and to be an attendee didn't merit a photograph. Claire searched the site until she came across a page of photographs taken at various conference functions. She found Damon and Sharon standing together at a cocktail party, apparently unaware of the camera. Damon wasn't looking at Sharon. In fact, he was smiling at another woman. No one was looking at Sharon, leaving her with no one else's expression to reflect. Her slouch and anxiety were all her own. Sometimes the camera caught truths the naked eye did not. Claire sent Damon and Sharon's image to the printer, too.

# Chapter Twenty-nine

She stood up to stretch her legs and go to the bathroom. By now it was late enough that the wrought iron gate separating CSWR from the main library was locked. Claire had to key in her code to leave without setting off the alarm. She notified the student on the Information Desk that she was taking a walk and would check in on her way back. A reference librarian waylaid her in the lobby to discuss their boss. It was always a guilty pleasure to bitch about Harrison and Claire lingered while the librarian complained.

When she passed by the Information Desk again the student said no one had been looking for her. Claire went to the gate and punched in her code to open it again. She walked down the hall to her office, opened the door, and had the disturbing sensation that she had stepped outside her body and was looking back at herself. There was a woman in the office wearing Claire's sage green cotton dress. The woman's back was turned and her head bent over the desk. It wasn't until she straightened up that Claire knew for sure it was Ansia. She hadn't realized when she gave away the dress how unsettling it would be to see Ansia wearing it. As Claire got older she discovered how women's fears changed with time. Fears that had once been projected outward became internalized. Once her greatest fear had been of the harm that men could inflict but tonight the fear that brought out the rats was of turning into a ranting, raving, drug-addicted woman who slept in the backseat of a junked car and peed on her clothes. Claire wanted to run from the image but this was her office. She saw a bouquet of wilted flowers lying on her desk, roses that were still red at the center but turning brown at the edges. If this was Ansia's gift, she should be thanked for it.

But first Claire asked, "Ansia? How did you get into my office? The gate was locked when I went out."

"I have the code," Ansia said. "Maia gave it to me."

That was a code Celia needed to change immediately without waiting for Seth to be chastised or tried by committee.

"The student at the Information Desk didn't see you?"

"Nobody saw me," Ansia said. She held out the skirt of the dress with one hand and made a curtsy. Claire accepted the gesture as a thank you.

"It looks good on you," she said. Ansia seemed to smell better in the dress. At least the office didn't reek of ammonia. "Thank you for coming. I have some pictures and one of them might be the woman who told you she was Maia's mother. Would you be willing to take a look?"

Ansia nodded.

Claire took the pictures she had printed and showed Jennifer Rule to Ansia.

"Her hair is too pretty," Ansia said. "That's not her."

Next Claire handed over the picture of Bettina and Bill Hartley accepting the triathlon trophy.

"That's the man who came," Ansia said. "Didn't I tell you he was a runner?"

"And the woman?" asked Claire. "Do you recognize her?"

"She's too young to be the woman I talked to," Ansia said. "She looks like a girl."

"She looks older in person," Claire said.

Ansia shook her head.

Ansia became so agitated when Claire handed her the picture of Sharon and Damon that the paper shook in her hands. She resembled a too-full bowl with a surface that remained smooth and tranquil when the bowl was held perfectly still, but the slightest push caused the liquid to churn and slosh over the edge. Claire assumed it was the sight of Sharon that brought on the anxiety, but Ansia was more interested in Damon.

"You know this man?" she asked.

"I've met him," Claire said.

"Does he work here?"

"No. He lives and works in Taos."

"I saw him here with Maia," Ansia said. "They were arguing on the steps."

"When?"

Ansia's eyes glazed over as she struggled to remember. Claire wondered if she was on drugs and if so, how long it had been since she shot up, how long it would be before she needed to shoot up again. "Right before Maia died. Is this man a john?"

"No. He's the man who abused Maia when she lived in Taos. He's to blame for her ending up on the street. Maia had agreed to tell the Taos County DA about him."

"Did he know that?"

"If he was arguing with her, I would say that he did. What about the woman? Do you recognize her?"

Ansia stared at Sharon's picture. "I don't know. The woman I saw was wearing a hat."

"Was she wearing glasses?"

"No." Ansia put the printouts down, went to the picture of the dancing girls on Claire's wall, and touched the shadow coming out of the corner of the painting. "That's him, isn't it?"

"I think it is," Claire replied.

"Men. They use you, abuse you, and leave you all tore up."

"These are nice flowers," Claire said,

picking up the roses, trying to calm Ansia by diverting her.

Ansia stared at the bouquet as if she had forgotten all about it. "They're for Maia. I found them in the Dumpster. I want to leave them here in the place where she died. Can I keep these pictures? They will help me remember."

"Sure," Claire said.

"Take me to the room where Maia died."

"It's supposed to be locked after hours," Claire replied.

"I have the code."

"It won't work. That room is used only for storage and it's locked with a dead bolt and a key."

Ansia shook her head, flapping the cherry red hair against her cheek. "Maia wouldn't sleep in a room like that," she insisted. "Take me there."

Claire agreed, hoping she would settle for leaving the flowers in the hallway outside the locked door. She handed the dead roses to Ansia, who put them and the printouts in a plastic bag. Claire led her to the elevator, wishing she could find some way to make both of them invisible. She didn't want to be seen taking Ansia into the basement. Technically CSWR was closed for the day, but people worked and studied in the library at all hours.

At every security door they came to, Claire

punched in her code. Once they stepped out of the elevator into the basement, the dullness left Ansia's eyes and she had the heightened awareness of a stalker conscious of every sound, every smell. It was the attitude that kept her alive on the street. If she had drugs in her system, Ansia seemed to have shaken them off.

They walked through the dim corridors where the pipes throbbed overhead. A red EXIT sign signaled escape to Claire but she walked right past it. They came to the closed door at the storage room.

"This is the room where Maia died," Claire said, not knowing what to do next. Hold hands? Sing a song? Say a prayer? Cry? "We could leave the flowers here and share our thoughts." It seemed lame, but it was the best she could come up with in the way of a ceremony.

"Let's go inside. I want to leave the flowers on the place where Maia died."

"The door is supposed to be locked," Claire said.

Ansia tried the handle. "It's not."

Claire was startled when the door opened and swung into the room. She reached around the corner and flipped the light switch, not wanting to step into the darkness. The overhead light revealed nothing new — stacks of empty boxes, shadows, dead roaches.

"I told you Maia wouldn't sleep in a locked room," Ansia said. "See what?" A rubber doorstop Claire hadn't noticed on her previous visit lay on the floor. Ansia kicked it.

Claire began to question everything Paul had said. They only had his word that the dead bolt to this door was routinely locked at night and over the weekend. Nobody else had ever cared or noticed. Claire's mind returned to her earlier question. Why bother to deadbolt a room that contained nothing of value?

"Show me the place she died," Ansia insisted.

Claire led her to the corner Paul had pointed out. "I was told the body was found here," she said.

Ansia dropped the flowers to the floor and knelt beside them. She took a candle from her plastic bag, lit it, and placed it on the floor next to the flowers. Claire saw it as a shrine to all "the girls who," a sad little *descanso* like the ones New Mexicans left beside the road in the places their loved ones died. Ansia bowed her head and Claire rested her hand on her shoulder. A shadow reached out from the hallway and fell over both of them.

# Chapter Thirty

Claire spun around and saw Paul Begala in his gray uniform standing in the doorway, holding a gym bag in his hand.

"What are you doing? You can't light a candle in here. You're not even allowed in here," he said. "No one's supposed to come here after hours."

Ansia's head was bent and her voice muffled. "Go away," she muttered.

"I thought the door wasn't supposed to be open after hours," Claire said.

"I had to work late fixing the leak but I'm going home now. I came by to lock the door."

Claire supposed he was going out through the library to the rear parking lot. His approach hadn't been preceded by the telltale jingle of his key ring or by his tuneless whistle. Claire didn't see any keys hanging from his belt, leading her to suspect he left the large key ring in his office when he went home and kept his office key on the same chain as his car and house keys. As he stood in the doorway and watched them, Paul's body was rigid with tension. But there was ambivalence in his mismatched eyes — hostility but also a worried, vulnerable quality that provided an opportunity. Detective Owen might be able to do it better, but Claire had the advantage of being here now.

"You don't routinely lock this door, do you?" she asked. "That's why Maia came in here to sleep."

Paul turned stubborn. "I always locked it. I told you already I didn't know she slept here."

"But somebody else did, and that person persuaded you to lock Maia in."

"I never talked to any woman claiming to be Maia's mother," Paul insisted.

"No, you talked to a man. Was it this man?"

Claire took the printouts from Ansia's plastic bag and stuck the picture of Damon in front of Paul's face. His instinctive reaction was to recoil from the image. His expression, full of fear and guilt, convinced Claire that he had spoken to Damon Fitzgerald, but law enforcement would need more. Detective Owen would have to follow rules of procedure when she questioned Paul, but Claire had entered a zone where the only rule was justice for Maia.

"I don't know him," Paul insisted. His tone was defiant, but neither eye would focus on Claire.

"His name is Damon Fitzgerald," she said. "He's an architect in Taos." Claire took a deep breath and stepped further into the lawless zone. "I believe he paid you to lock Maia in the storage room for the weekend." Ansia remained huddled in the corner, watching the conversational volley with eyes bouncing from Claire to Paul.

"Why would he do that?" Paul asked.

"He's under investigation for criminal sexual penetration," Claire said. "Maia intended to testify against him. His intent was to stop her." Remembering that Paul was a man who liked to fish in mountain streams, a man who took care of his ailing wife, a man who had to have a soft side, Claire lowered her voice and said, "It would be better for you if you told the truth. There is a witness who saw Damon here arguing with Maia right before she died." Claire was relieved when Ansia did not identify herself as that witness. "There are other witnesses who knew Damon's girlfriend was looking for Maia. I'm sure you only got involved because your wife needed help." Claire had switched from bad cop to good with a finesse Detective Owen might have admired. "The DA will understand that. It's Damon she's after, not you. If you can help her prosecute him, she will be lenient."

Paul focused his blue eye on Claire as he said, "Well, whatever happened here you can blame that guy for it. He told me he wanted to keep the girl locked up for a few days to straighten her out. That's all. He gave me a bag with food and water and a waste bucket. I left them in the room where she would find them. Was that a crime? He said he was Maia's stepfather. He was going up to Taos to get her mother, he told me. He was afraid Maia would run away again. He said he'd be back on Saturday or Sunday and would call me. He wanted to be there when I opened the door. I gave him my cell number. If he'd called I'da come in at any time. How was I supposed to know the girl would bring drugs into the room with her?"

"She didn't," Claire said. "Damon or his girlfriend put the drugs in the bag with the food."

"You're telling me that guy deliberately locked his stepdaughter up with heroin?"

No, he provided the heroin and you locked her up, Claire thought, but she didn't say so. Now that she had Paul talking, she didn't want to stop the flow.

"His girlfriend was trading China White for information on the street. Damon had to know that locked up in a room with the drug, Maia would take it; she was a reformed addict and she was claustrophobic. The heroin was very fine and very dangerous."

"Why would he want to kill his own stepdaughter?" Paul asked.

"She wasn't his stepdaughter. He was once her mother's lover and then he abused Maia when she was only twelve years old. That's the case the DA was investigating. Maia was going to testify against Damon for a first-degree felony that could have put him in jail for life."

Ansia had been huddling in the corner so still that Claire had almost forgotten she was there. But she jumped up now and cried out, "How much did you get for killing Maia?" in a hoarse voice.

"I didn't kill nobody. All I did was lock the door," Paul said. "She killed herself."

"How much did you get for that?" Ansia demanded.

"A couple of thousand," Paul admitted.

It was a huge sum of money to Ansia, a mountain of drugs, but nothing at all to Damon's heiress girlfriend. It had to be a very small amount, taking into consideration that it was intended to keep Damon out of prison, where a child abuser's life was worthless. It was only a drop in the bucket of the long-term costs of caring for Paul's wife but it should have been more than enough to tell him he was doing something very, very wrong.

"You bastard, you killed Maia for a couple of thousand dollars." Ansia's emotions boiled over. "You're no better than a candy man on the street."

"I didn't kill her," Paul protested.

"You did." Ansia opened her plastic bag,

pulled out an object, and lunged at Paul.

"What the hell are you doing?" he yelled.

Claire's mind had the slow-motion clarity that precedes disaster. The flash of metal she saw wasn't the dull blade of the paring knife she had given Ansia. It was the sharp glint of a hunting knife large enough to skin and dismember an animal. Ansia lives in a parked car, Claire thought. Of course she carries a knife.

Paul dropped his bag and put his arm up to protect his face. Ansia raised the knife and slashed the arm, releasing a stream of blood.

Claire pulled the skirt of the green dress and tried to stop her. "Ansia, don't!"

Ansia lifted the knife and lunged again, and the fabric ripped loose in Claire's hands. The knife sliced Paul across the shoulder, drawing more blood. He groaned and sank down to the floor. As Ansia pounced on him, he kicked his bag between her feet, tripping her. The knife fell out of her hand and clattered across the floor. Claire had a split second to decide whether to go for the woman or the knife. Fearing a knife would be useless in her hands, she knelt over Ansia and pinned her to the floor. Ansia squirmed and bucked, trying to throw her off, but Claire held tight.

"Are you all right?" she asked Paul.

"I don't know," he said in a dazed voice.

"Where's your cell phone?"

"In the office."

"Can you get up and call for help?"

"I'll try," Paul said.

"Do it. I can't hold her for long." The bloody knife lay on the floor. If Claire didn't get it, Paul would, but she was afraid of what Ansia would do if she let go. She might get to the knife first. She might attack Paul again. The knife had to be safer in his hands than in hers. Paul had people he had to answer to, but Ansia was responsible to no one, not even herself.

"Don't let him get it." She squirmed and kicked at Claire.

"Take it now," Claire said to Paul. "Get out of here. Get help."

He pushed himself off the floor, picked up the knife, and stood beside them, clutching the handle. All it would take to get himself out of this mess would be to raise his arm, stab both of them to death, and leave the knife in Ansia's hand. The question was whether he was physically or emotionally capable of such brutality. Claire believed that you never knew what people were capable of until they were put in a situation that brought out their best — or their worst. The room was so still she heard the pipes throbbing like an artery.

"It's only a matter of time before the APD learns about you," she said. "I've told my associates everything I know. If you go to prison for killing us, how can you help your wife?"

Paul stared at the knife until the blood ran down his arm and onto the blade. He walked out of the room and down the hall. Claire was faced with what to do about Ansia, who had stopped squirming and stared at her with listless eyes.

"I need your help," Claire said. "If you can identify Damon and the woman who gave you the China White, you can put both of them in prison for a long, long time. You'll get a chance to see the woman in a lineup wearing a hat and dressed as she was when you met her. You can't go back on the street now; you won't be safe. You want those people to be punished for killing Maia, don't you?"

Ansia nodded. The fight had gone out of her. Her body twitched. "I need *mi medicina*," she whispered.

In prison she was all too likely to find her *medicina*, but the court might put her into rehab instead. She would have to be drug-free to testify, and she would have to testify in order to convict Damon.

Claire looked down at the sage green dress smeared with dirt and blood. "Many girls have been hurt by men," she said, "and too many men have gotten away with it. But you have the chance to punish the man who killed Maia and hurt the other girls. You're the only one who can. It will be hard, but it will be worth it. Promise me you won't run away if I let you go. Promise me you'll stay here and talk to the police when they come. Say you'll do it for Maia."

Ansia nodded. It was her chance to be a hero.

"I'll be your *medicina*," Claire said. She helped Ansia into a sitting position, leaned against the wall, and rocked her in her arms until the police showed up.

# Chapter Thirty-one

Paul Begala recovered from Ansia's wounds. He was fired from his job at UNM but he found another at the nursing home that cared for his wife. Ansia was charged with assault with a deadly weapon. Unable to raise bail she was held over for trial. Detective Owen told Claire that this could be considered a good thing. Prison would keep Ansia safe until the time came to testify she'd seen June Reid arguing with Damon Fitzgerald. Convicting her of assault would get her off the street at least for a while. Detective Owen pulled some strings and got Ansia admitted to a special treatment program for female drug addicts. Drugs were almost as easy to come by in prison as they were on the street, but this program isolated the women from the general prison population and kept them drug-free. Claire agreed the program would be beneficial but she wasn't sure Ansia would see it that way.

The Bernalillo County prosecutor was convinced that Damon had demonstrated the malice aforethought and cool reflection that made it possible to charge him with murder in the first degree in the death of June Reid.

There was no physical evidence to link him, no evidence that June hadn't brought the heroin into the storage room herself, only the testimony of Paul Begala, Ansia, and eventually Sharon Miller. The prosecutor did not have a great case against Sharon. Her disguises made it difficult for the people she talked to — Ansia, Seth Malcolm, and Linda Butler — to positively identify her, even when dressed appropriately in a police lineup. But the prosecutor chipped away at Sharon's resolve. Her fear of a long jail sentence proved stronger than her devotion to Damon Fitzgerald and eventually she gave him up, declaring that the plan had been his and that he was the one who purchased the China White in San Francisco. Sharon claimed she didn't know the heroin was special in any way, that she didn't know it would kill anyone, that she never knew Damon's intent was to kill June Reid. She thought he just waned to find her and talk to her.

When Detective Owen called to tell Claire about Sharon's testimony, Claire asked if she believed her.

"I do," Owen said.

"Her story seems rather self-serving to me," Claire said.

"Yes, but that doesn't mean it's not true. Sharon's not a very good actress or a very convincing liar. I think she was just dumb enough to fall for the wrong guy. What is it that attracts women to these creative types?"

"They cat out something the women are unwilling or unable to express themselves."

"Maybe Sharon wanted to be a creative person, maybe even a wild person, but we found nothing in her background to indicate she was vicious enough to be a killer. On the other hand, there is plenty of criminal activity in Damon's background. One thing we see over and over again is that it's not that big a step from abuser to killer. We've got enough on Damon that his career as an abuser is over."

"I hope so," Claire said.

"Trust me," Owen said.

Once Damon was incarcerated in Albuquerque, Sophie Roybal came forward and said she'd be willing to testify against him for criminal sexual penetration in Taos. The Bernalillo County prosecutor said her testimony might be useful in the homicide trial, but Allana Bruno had become far more interested in reopening the case of Veronica Reid's death than in trying to convict Damon of criminal sexual penetration. If Damon had been involved in the apparent overdose death of June Reid, it was reasonable to ask whether he'd also been involved in the apparent suicide of her mother. Claire thought that in one sense Damon had followed the path of a serial abuser who continued inflicting harm until all the victims were dead. When Allana Bruno began to question members of the Cave Commune, looking for a way to link Damon to Veronica's death, he said he could produce evidence that would exonerate him. The evidence was a letter postmarked Taos on the day Veronica died.

"You are responsible for this," the letter read. "My life is a black hole I can't climb out of. I don't want to go on living anymore and I blame you. You are a monster who seduced my daughter and turned her against me. You have ruined her life and you have ruined mine. I hate you. Veronica."

The letter wasn't delivered until the day after Veronica was found dead in the gorge, too late, Damon said, for him to have prevented her from killing herself. He could have solved the mystery of her death and eased people's minds by releasing the letter when he received it, but that would have been another blow to his battered image. Assisted suicide — helping someone who had chosen to die — was a crime in New Mexico. It wasn't a crime for a man to be so wantonly cruel that his lovers chose the path of killing themselves.

There were many who blamed Damon for Veronica's death even though he was never charged with that crime. Veronica died several years before her daughter so she couldn't be held responsible for June's death, but

Claire saw blame there, too. She couldn't disagree with Maureen Prescott's assessment that Veronica should have hung on for her daughter's sake. For her to blame everything on Damon and to leave her daughter unprotected was to take the easy way out.

Damon and Sharon's house was searched for evidence during the murder investigations, but the original of *Summertime* was never found. Claire came to believe that one or both of them had destroyed it. It disturbed her that such a beautiful painting could vanish. Having a computer-generated copy was not even close to having the original. Before she called Lisa Teague to tell her the painting had been lost, Claire took her copy of *Summertime* down from her wall and put it away.

"I'm sorry to hear it wasn't at the house," Lisa said, "but it might turn up somewhere else."

"It might," Claire replied.

Lisa didn't sound terribly disappointed. Claire suspected that, as she'd said, she cut her emotional connection to *Summertime* when she gave the painting over to the Downtown Gallery. Her ability to remove herself from her artwork made Claire wonder if she wouldn't turn out to be a social worker after all. It was hard to imagine Edward Girard ever disconnecting from the work he created.

"I've decided on a painting I'd like to own," Claire told Lisa.

"Excellent. Which one?"

When Claire told her, Lisa asked, "Are you sure?"

"Yes."

"Okay. I have a class tomorrow. I can bring it to your office in the afternoon."

Lisa showed up with the painting wrapped in brown paper. Before she began to unwrap it, she looked at the white space on Claire's wall and said, "You could use a painting in here," she said, "but are you sure this is the one you want?"

"I'm sure," Claire said.

"Okay. The gallery originally put a price on it of seven hundred and fifty dollars. Even at that price it didn't sell, so they marked it down to five hundred dollars."

"That had nothing to do with the quality of the painting."

"I know. It's the subject that turns people off. If you want to pay the gallery the mark-down price, that'll be all right. I can drop the check off on my way home."

Claire took out her checkbook and wrote out a check for twenty-five hundred dollars to the gallery while Lisa unwrapped the painting.

"That's very generous," Lisa said when she saw the amount. "Chris will be thrilled."

"It's worth it," Claire replied.

They found the perfect spot on the white wall and hung the painting there, adjusting it until it was symmetrical. Then Lisa said good-bye and rushed off to her class.

Claire was left with an image of a woman in a gauzy white dress hugging the curves of a river like smoke with her red hair floating behind her. She knew Harrison wouldn't approve, but she didn't let that stop her. It was her life. Her office. Her wall.

It took time to get used to Ansia's presence. Claire would forget about the painting when she was working, then look up to see the cherry red hair, the sinuous river, the attenuated body. It was an image that incorporated elements of escapism, but it was also raw, bold, and honest.

"Did I hang that?" Claire asked herself.

"You did," she answered.

"Whoa!" Celia said the first time she walked through the doorway and saw it on the wall. "Where did *that* come from?"

"I bought it from Lisa Teague. The money goes to Hope Central Shelter."

"Has Harrison complained?"

"Not yet, but he scowls every time he walks by and looks in my window, and Harrison never walks down the hall without looking in my window."

"It's Ansia on drugs, right?"

"Right."

"Well, at least she's not wearing your dress.

Of all of Lisa's paintings, why did you pick that one? It's going to be hard to forget what happened with that on the wall."

"I don't want to forget," Claire said. "I want to be reminded of how raw life can be outside our ivory tower." It was her hope that one day, when Ansia was released from prison, she would come by and take pride in visiting her image on the wall. She hoped that Ansia would be cleaned up, odor free, and off drugs at that time, but she would be welcome even if she was not.

Celia gave Claire the kind of penetrating stare she had come to expect from Detective Owen. Claire stared back at her until Celia shrugged and said, "Okay. It's your wall. What are you planning to do with the Spiral Rocks illustration once the police return it?"

"It will be inserted into *Ancient Sites*, but the book won't be the same, which raises the question of what to do with the book. If we put it back on the shelf it will just be another damaged first edition."

"Now it's a book with a story connected to it, a story that could eventually become a legend. That should make it even more valuable," Celia said.

"I'm going to suggest we put it in a glass case and display it with other legendary books."

"Sounds good." Celia picked up a paperweight from Claire's desk and balanced it in the palm of her hand. "The security committee had a meeting with Harrison and came to a decision about Seth."

Claire suspected that decision had been a foregone conclusion, but she waited to hear what Celia had to say.

She put the paperweight down and made the motion of a blade slicing across her neck. "He's out of here," Celia said. "He broke the rules. His code has been retired for good. Seth can no longer do research at CSWR. He lost his fellowship. He will not be getting his doctorate on Tobiah James at UNM. All the work he has done so far has gone for naught."

"He stopped by to ask if there was anything I could do to help," Claire said.

"There wasn't," Celia replied. "Harrison's mind was made up."

"I know." Claire was left with more sympathy for Seth than anyone else at CSWR had.

Damon Fitzgerald was in prison and all the pieces seemed to be in place to keep him there for a long time. Claire was glad that her persistence in standing up for Maia had helped. It relieved some of the guilt she had carried around about not exposing George Hogan. She should have been sleeping well but she woke up in the middle of the night hearing moths fluttering in the darkness —

the spirits of the dead, she thought, no longer the unnotified next of kin. The DNA test proved Edward Girard was June's father. He buried her in a sad little ceremony at Spiral Rocks.

It bothered Claire that unlike her mother, June had left no note. No one would ever know what her last thoughts and words were. Did she know or suspect that Damon was the one responsible for locking her in with the China White? Did she inject the drug intending to kill herself or only to escape from the claustrophobic room? What were her final thoughts about her mother, her father, and Damon Fitzgerald, the adults who should have put her best interests first but never did.

In the middle of a clear night when the stars were diamonds in the sky, Claire took her leather-bound journal from her nightstand and composed a note on June's behalf.

> I'm alone. The door is locked. No one can hear my screams. The walls are closing in. The people who should have looked out for me didn't. It will be so hard to go back to Taos and testify against Damon. I wish Bill Hartley had never tracked me down and asked me. Damon didn't rape me. I was willing but I was young and stupid. Damon ruled at

Cave Commune. The ultimate responsibility is his. He needs to be stopped before he can hurt any more girls, and I am the only one who can stop him. I have to do it for all the girls. I'm going to take this heroin so I can stay calm until someone comes to rescue me. June Reid.

It was a possible note, but not the only one. In the middle of another, darker night, when only the brightest stars were visible and clouds scudded across the moon, Claire wrote:

Damon became a bear who assaulted me. I can't face him ever again. Bill Hartley has no right to ask me to do it. I'll tell him I can never go back to Taos. Someone deliberately put heroin in the food bag and it didn't come from Albuquerque. It's too white, too pure, too dangerous. It will kill me if I take it. Sooner or later someone will open the door and let me out.

But time passed, nobody came, and that changed to:

No one's coming. I can't stand it anymore. I am going to be with my mother.

After she wrote that ending Claire got up and paced around her house with the lights off.

* * *

The morning after she wrote the second note she made herself a cup of coffee, went into her office, and checked her E-mail to find a short but lovely note from Pietro Antonelli.

> Clara, My daughter and I are planning a trip to California next month to look at schools for her. Could we visit you in Albuquerque while we are in the West? It would be wonderful to see you again. Love, Pietro.

"Of course you can visit," Claire wrote back. "I'd be delighted. I'm looking forward to seeing you again and to meeting your daughter. Love, Clara."

The upcoming visit from Pietro and his daughter gave life an anticipatory buzz. Claire still woke up in the middle of the night, but she had something light to look forward to as well as something dark to forget.

One evening as she watched *Star Gazer* with Jack Horkheimer on PBS she learned that the constellation Pleiades could be seen at the tip of the horn of Taurus, the bull, near Orion, the hunter. The horns of Taurus were easy to find that particular night because they were wrapped around the new moon.

"Keep looking up!" Jack Horkheimer advised at the end of the show.

Claire turned off the TV and went outside. With guidance from Jack she was able to locate the cluster of the seven sisters who huddled together as they roamed the sky. If the night skies were totally black and the stars had never existed, she believed that human beings would have had to invent them. The constellations symbolized so perfectly the passions and imperfections of human beings. Claire felt that if she wrote one more note before she went to bed, she might be able to sleep through the night. On Maia's behalf she wrote in her journal:

> I have been sleeping here for months, but no one has ever locked the door on me. I am terrified, but I have my illustration with the rocks pointing toward the sky. There is white to smooth the way. I am Maia. I am leaving this place to join my beautiful sisters. We are the stars who light the sky.

# About the Author

***Judith Van Gieson*** is the author of two mystery series, one featuring rare book expert Claire Reynier and the other featuring lawyer and sleuth Neil Hamel. Ms. Van Gieson lives in Albuquerque, New Mexico. Visit her on the Web at www.judithvangieson.com.